# Wounded DANCE

**Book 2 of the Lovers Dance Series**

---

**by Deanna Roy**

Six-Time *USA Today* bestselling author of

*The Forever Series*

*The Lovers Dance Series*

---

Sign up to be notified about new releases via email or text.

This is a work of fiction. All the characters, organizations, and events portrayed in this novel are either products of the author's imagination or used fictitiously.

Casey Shay Press
PO Box 160116
Austin, TX 78716
www.caseyshaypress.com

E-ISBN: 9781938150647
Paperback ISBN: 9781938150630

Library of Congress Control Number: 2017901094
eBook version 3.0

## Summary

When the man from Livia's past returns to claim what he believes to be his, Blitz and Livia must bind themselves more tightly than ever to survive the storm.

Get emails or texts from Deanna about her new releases:
Deanna's List

~*´♥`*~

*To superfans*
*Christine A and Jennifer P*
*for being early readers*
*for the crazy plot twist*
*and providing the names*
*Denham and Jenica*

# Chapter One

These are the best days.

Gabriella leans sideways in her wheelchair, arm curved over her shiny black hair. Even at four years old, her ballet movements show expression and deep emotion.

She is her mother's daughter, even if she doesn't realize it. She may never know that I gave birth to her and spent years searching for her. I'm okay with that. Teaching her ballet is a joy.

Her pale pink tutu is brilliant with sparkles. It matches mine, minus the glitter. When I glance in the wall of mirrors behind the barre, my long black hair blending into hers, I don't see how anyone could miss that we are related.

But so far, she's a perfect secret.

"Hold," I tell her, and shift her fingers into a prettier position.

"Good call," Blitz says. He's standing nearby, his hand cupping his scruffy chin, watching Gabriella's movements with an eye toward improvement. He wants to maximize the ways she can dance from the wheelchair.

You'd never guess this patient man, who seems to have all the time in the world, is actually Blitz Craven, currently the most famous dancer in the world due to his reality TV show *Dance Blitz*.

I turn toward the mirrored window to the hall outside. I can't see through it, but I know Gabriella's adopted mother Gwen is watching. She's been a good mother to my baby, strong and caring even after the car accident that killed her husband and damaged our little girl's spine.

After I told Blitz about my secret daughter, he suggested we give her private lessons. I changed my life to be near her, and now he has too.

Gwen was delighted at the idea of extra dance help, especially from someone as famous as Blitz. So now I get to see Gabriella twice each week. Once in her class for all the wheelchair ballerinas. And again during the lesson with me and Blitz.

Gwen doesn't know who I am. No one does. My

parents, whom I haven't seen in the month since I left home to be with Blitz, don't know I found her.

For a year, my discovery of her was my own solitary secret. Then I told Blitz just a few weeks ago, at the Christmas dance recital.

Now the new year has begun and it's off to an amazing start. Blitz and I are staying at a hotel close by, still hoping my parents will come around and be willing to speak to me again.

Blitz and I dance together at Dreamcatcher every day while the producers of his show *Dance Blitz* manage the publicity following my surprise arrival and Blitz's unscripted announcement on live television that I was his new dance partner. His manager Hannah still hasn't calmed down about it.

Right now things are easy and good. I miss my little brother Andy, and since he is homeschooled like I used to be, I can't easily see him. But I've been up to my church and managed to tell him hello and give him a hug before my parents took him away.

"Let's try something with a quicker tempo," Blitz says, heading toward the audio equipment in the corner. "Gabriella, are you getting tired?"

The little girl whizzes across the room. "No way! This is the best!"

She whirls in circles as Blitz starts a new song. We let her lead a little conga line with me and Blitz behind her, then Blitz gives her a ribbon stick to practice with.

I take a step back to watch them. Blitz is wearing sleek black jazz pants and a tight gray dance shirt. He takes my breath away. His hair has grown out a little and falls in a black wave across his head. Despite living with him for over a month, I still don't know how he manages to keep his sexy stubble at precisely the same length all the time.

He catches me watching him and winks, showing Gabriella how to make a rapid cascade with the ribbon. Seeing them together never fails to fill my heart with unabashed joy.

The lights flicker, signaling that the hour is ending. Another group will use this room next.

Blitz takes Gabriella's ribbon stick and rolls it up. She speeds across the room to make a circle around me. Her chair is good, light and nimble. There is a lot she will be able to do.

Gwen opens the door and peeks inside. "All done?" she asks.

She looks happier now that she's made it through the holidays. It's not the first one without her husband, but I imagine it's not much better yet. It will probably never be easy for her. She approaches Gabriella with a hot-pink coat.

"Thank you guys so much for doing this," she says. "Gabby, you looked so good. Was it fun?"

Gabriella sticks her arms in the coat. "It was!" She tries to zip it up herself, but like many four-year-olds, she's not agile enough. Gwen leans over to fasten it for her, one of a million small acts of mothering I will never get to do.

"I will see you on Tuesday for the big class," I tell her, leaning down for a hug. She smells like strawberry shampoo. It's hard to let her go, and especially to hide how I'm feeling, but I straighten and keep my expression friendly and light.

"Bye, Livia!" Gabriella calls. "Bye, Benjamin!"

Gwen waves to us and follows Gabriella out of the room.

I bite my lip to stay in control and turn to Blitz. "I should probably call you Benjamin too," I say. "It's the rest of the world who knows you as Blitz."

He walks up and wraps his arms around me, resting his chin on my head. "You can call me anything you want."

"Don't tempt me," I say with a laugh. "I can come up with all manner of depraved nicknames."

He pulls back and presses a light kiss on my mouth. Then he says, "I like it when you're depraved."

He spins me out in a whirl, his hand and body

communicating where I should go. For a few dizzying seconds, we dance together in dramatic turns, the world a blur. Then he pulls me against him, our bodies flush against each other.

A lot of our conversations end like this.

"Lunch?" I ask him, breathing hard.

He laughs. "Absolutely."

I head to the corner where I've stashed my coat and a bag with normal shoes.

He heads for the sound equipment. "Make sure you save room for dinner, though. Mom will expect you to eat!"

My stomach flutters. Tonight I'll be meeting Blitz's parents for the first time. We would have done it before now, but they spent Christmas and early January in Colorado, so they've just now gotten back and settled down enough to have visitors.

Blitz shuts down the music as Aurora arrives to set up for her toddler class. She has a little girl with her, Cassandra, her boyfriend's daughter.

"You have a helper!" I say to Aurora.

"No school today," Aurora says. "I'm watching her while Samuel works." Her eyes flit over to Blitz. Even though he volunteered here for a few weeks around Thanksgiving last year, everyone is still a little starstruck when they see him.

It's been worse since the live finale of his show,

which went completely viral and has been the highest-rated reality show episode of all time. My face still flushes when I think of how bold I was to march on that stage and demand he dance with me instead of the contestants.

Sometimes my friend Mindy sends me memes of a screenshot from the broadcast. It shows me crossing in front of the three finalists in their sparkly dresses. I look grim and determined. The captions are always changing.

*What a hostile takeover looks like.*

*When you ain't gonna let no ho dance with your man.*

I try to ignore all the fuss. Blitz and I want to live as quietly as we can for as long as possible, at least until we can figure out what's next. I know the finalists from his show feel robbed and angry. One of them, Mariah, has sued the producers, since she was supposedly slated to be the actual winner. She lost out on a lot of publicity and fame because of me.

It's a mess.

Blitz takes my hand as I stand up from putting on my shoes. We head down the hall of Dreamcatcher Dance Academy, which is filling with moms and little girls for their classes. There's more kids here today with school out, siblings of the tiny ones who usually attend alone. The mothers seem more harried than usual.

We cross the foyer, waving at Suze, who sits at the front desk. A few moms stop talking to point at Blitz. He smiles and is friendly, but doesn't pause, his hand on my back as we head for the doors.

I'm on the steps when my brain stutters. My attention fixes on a man on the sidewalk, looking up, his cheeks ruddy from the cold as if he's stood there a while.

My body gets some message from my brain before I can comprehend exactly what is happening, why I'm feeling a threat. My feet are rooted to the concrete, my chest buzzing with alarm.

Blitz stops with me. "You okay, Livia?" he asks.

His words are what bring the moment into focus. This man in front of me wears a black leather jacket, his layered brown hair flying in the wind.

It's him.

God.

It's him.

Denham Young.

Kicked out of my life when I was fifteen. Gone for good. Lost to me.

My great love. My shame.

Gabriella's father.

He's found me.

## Chapter Two

Denham takes a step toward me, then sees Blitz and stops. "Livia, it's really you."

I want to shrink into the ground, let it swallow me up. I can't let Blitz meet him. I can't let Denham say who he is. If Blitz knew, that would be it. He would be horrified. He wouldn't want me anymore. And the press. I'm famous now. If they knew. God. Everyone would know. It would be huge news.

And Denham...he doesn't know about Gabriella. At least I don't think so. My father kicked him out before I found out I was pregnant. We didn't see him again.

I look wildly across the parking lot. Thankfully Gwen has already gone.

Why is this happening?

"Livia?" Denham says.

"Go away!" I cry out. "Stay back!"

With that, Blitz pulls me close to him. "Who is this guy, Livia? You want me to take his ass out?"

"No!" I say. "Just get me out of here."

"Livia, please, there is something I have to tell you!" Denham says. He holds his arms out in a pleading gesture. His face, God, that face, one I knew as well as my own, is contorted in anguish.

"No!" I say. "I don't want to hear it! Please, stay away!"

Blitz hurries us toward his car on the far side of the building.

But Denham follows. "I couldn't find you, Livia, or I would have told you sooner. I looked everywhere! I didn't know where you had gone until I saw you on television!"

Blitz stops beside his car and whirls around, pushing me behind him. "Look, pal, get out of here before your face is part of the pavement. Livia doesn't want to talk to you. Just because she was on the show doesn't mean you have the right to stalk her."

Blitz jerks his keys from his pocket and unlocks the door. "Get in, Livia," he says.

But my feet are stuck. Denham looks so stricken. He's older now, and so am I. We're grown. He isn't that fresh-faced sixteen-year-old. But his eyes are the same. I'd been lost in them once. Lost enough to forget to be careful. I didn't guard myself.

But he lied. He led me to my shame.

This gets me.

I manage to turn away and jerk open the door to Blitz's red Ferrari. The wind tears at my coat and my hair swirls around my face.

"Livia," Denham says. "Just let me say one thing."

I pause by the door and look back. Blitz is still next to him, looking threatening and angry. I've seen Blitz take down a stranger with a single punch. I have no doubt he'd do it again.

"Please," I say. "Please don't come into my life now. I can't bear it."

Denham's face is contorted with emotion. "I won't. I see you've got a good thing going." He glances at Blitz. "I wouldn't mess that up. I promise. I would never hurt you. I loved you more than anyone else in the world. More than I will ever love anybody again."

This makes Blitz relax his stance. He looks back at me. "Livia, who is this?" he asks.

My panic rises. "I'll tell you in the car," I say. But I don't get in. I can't leave Denham and Blitz alone, even for a second. In fact, I need Blitz away from this situation, as fast as possible, before Denham can say anything more.

"Can we go now?" I ask him, my voice quavering.

If Denham says who he is, this is over. My life is over. I will tell Blitz that Denham is Gabriella's father. I don't care about that.

It's the rest. Who he is to *me*. To my family.

But Blitz waits, looking back and forth between me and Denham.

I close my eyes to the wind, trying to stay calm, not to scream and run. This is it. This is where my past catches up to me.

"I'm leaving," I say to Denham one last time. "Blitz, please, let's drive away."

This time, Blitz moves. He comes around to the driver's side of the car and opens the door, his eyes still on Denham.

But Denham is determined to say something. And so he does. And the words are something I never thought I'd hear.

"Livia, I'm not your brother. I never was."

## Chapter Three

I clutch the top of Blitz's car. The wind is fierce. Surely I didn't hear that right.

"What?" Blitz says. "You're her brother?"

Denham steps closer. "No, I said I'm *not* her brother. She thought I was. Hell, *I* thought I was. I lived with her family. But I'm not part of it."

I can't look at him. My world is spinning, black spots in my vision.

He takes yet another step. He's only a couple feet away now. My head is down because I can't look anybody in the eye right now. His boots are scuffed and worn, a chain across the side. He still dresses with an attitude, now the same as then.

"Livia?" Blitz's voice is laced with concern. He comes back around the car. "You lived with this guy?"

"Not here in San Antonio," Denham says. "Back in Houston. I didn't know she was here. I had no idea where she was until the show."

Blitz's arms come around me. His voice is gentle. "Hey, what's getting you? Did this guy do something to you when you lived with him?"

I shake my head no, then yes, then no again. Blitz's arms are like a tether to the world. I finally lift my face.

Denham's arms are out again, like he's begging. His eyes are soft. "I'm not your brother," he says again. "After your father kicked me out, I went into foster care. I ran away, but they had already DNA-swabbed me to hand me over to some other guy they found. I never went back, so I didn't see the results. I saw the papers a year ago, when Aunt Didi died. Your dad isn't my dad. But I couldn't find you to tell you. That we were okay. That it wasn't anything horrible after all."

Now I'm feeling faint. He has to stop. "Please take me home," I say to Blitz. "Now."

Blitz nods and steps between me and Denham, blocking his view of me as I sit on the seat. I've heard all I need to know. I just need to think. And I need to get away before the last piece of the story falls into place for both of them.

But this isn't my scene. It's Denham's. And he is going to say what he wants.

"I always loved you, Livia," Denham goes on. "And I never regretted what happened between us. I wanted you to be able to stop regretting it too."

Blitz still stands by my open door. His face is lowered, but I can see him thinking. "Is this the guy?" he asks me. "The one who got you pregnant?"

My head snaps around to look at Denham.

His eyes get wide. "What?" Denham asks. "What is he saying?"

Blitz realizes the situation and tries to close the door.

But Denham steps forward and grabs it. "Livia? Did you get pregnant?"

I want the car to collapse around me, crush me into a cube to be tossed into a pit. This moment must end. It's all come together. Blitz. Denham. Gabriella. My brother who isn't my brother after all.

"Let me get this straight," Blitz says. "You," he says, pointing at Denham, "were her brother but now you're not."

"Half-brother," Denham says. He's still trying to get past Blitz to me. "And she didn't know. I moved in when I was sixteen."

Blitz's voice is low and menacing. "She knew at

some point, or you wouldn't be telling her the truth now."

Denham looks at Blitz. "Her dad made me keep the secret or I couldn't move in. If I told, then Livia's mother would know he had been unfaithful."

Blitz lets out a rush of air. "So Livia, MY Livia, was seduced by you, when you were living there as her brother."

Denham tries to look around Blitz again. "When I thought I was. But I'm not. Livia, tell me about the baby."

Blitz won't let it go. "And you didn't think to tell her that little detail? When you were *sleeping* with her?" He looks like he might punch Denham after all.

Denham gets increasingly agitated. "I loved her. I just wanted to protect her from what people would think."

Blitz grips the door frame so hard his knuckles are white.

"*I* think," Blitz says, then pauses. "No, I *know*, that you seduced a very young girl living in your house, by all accounts your half-sister. And you didn't even prevent her from getting pregnant."

"That is past," Denham says. He's done with Blitz. I can hear it in his voice. He tries to shoulder Blitz out of the way.

"Where is our baby, Livia?" Denham asks. "You're

Catholic, so I know you had it." He leans down to get closer to my face. "WHERE IS OUR BABY?"

And that's when Blitz slams his elbow against the back of Denham's neck.

Denham crumples to the ground.

## Chapter Four

"Blitz!" I cry. But I don't try to get out of the car or help Denham. I can't do that. My allegiance is with Blitz. It has to be.

My mind is a whirl. Denham isn't my brother. My father was lied to. We all were.

It's too much. I take great gulps of air while Blitz nudges Denham with his foot, waiting for him to come around. He's out cold on the pavement by the door. Thankfully no one's in the parking lot of the academy right now to see.

"How did you know where to hit him?" I ask Blitz.

Blitz barks out a sardonic laugh. "That's what you're thinking about right now?"

I look down at Denham. The space over his eye is

swelling a little where he hit the door of the car on the way down.

"The rest is too much for me right now," I say. I'm barely holding it together. I have to get past this moment with Denham on the ground, and Blitz in an angry posture over him. I have to get away so I can sort all this out.

"I was supposed to be on some action TV show," Blitz says. "*Artists and Outlaws*. We were dancers who fought crime. Dumbest premise on the face of the earth. We shot a pilot but nobody took it. I had to train in combat for it."

This random conversation helps my mind settle. "I'm sorry the show didn't happen."

"I'm not," Blitz says. "Probably would have destroyed my career."

Denham shifts his arm and groans.

"Lover boy is back," Blitz says. "What do you want me to do with him?"

"Move him out of the way so we can leave?" I say, more of a question than a suggestion.

"All right," Blitz says. He bends down to drag Denham away from the car, but Denham shakes his head and rolls over.

He presses his hand to his forehead. "Damn, dance boy," he says. "I didn't figure on you being a heavy."

"I figured on you being an asshole," Blitz says. "I should have done it sooner."

Denham struggles to his feet, his hand on the back of his neck. He takes a step toward me, but Blitz moves in again.

Denham holds up his hands. "All right, all right. Simmer down." He tilts his head so he can see me around Blitz's body. "This isn't over, Livia. I'm going to find that baby."

He glances up at the giant letters of Dreamcatcher Dance Academy. "And I know where to find y'all."

Denham turns and stumbles off. He opens the door to a beat-up dark green pickup truck and sits down.

Blitz closes my door and walks around. We wait a moment until Denham starts his truck and screeches off down the street.

"You okay?" Blitz asks. He reaches for my hand and lifts my fingers to his lips.

I manage to nod. I'm so scared he will be freaked out by what he's learned about me. Nobody's ever known who Gabriella's father is, except my parents. They wouldn't even tell the doctor, and I knew from eighth-grade science that a baby from related people could have problems.

But we weren't related. It had all been a lie.

I shake my head. So much to sort out. I want to talk to my parents, but they aren't speaking to me right now.

And...as for parents, I am supposed to meet Blitz's in a few hours.

Is that still on?

Is *he* still on?

His warm lips against my fingers seem to indicate we are fine. I glance over at him. He watches me with concern. "You want to talk about it now?" he asks.

I don't, but I know I have to.

"Denham showed up one summer, a couple months before my fifteenth birthday," I say. "His aunt brought him. Didi. She was old and pretty sick. And Denham was wild. His mother had not been very involved in his life and had overdosed on something. Her heart stopped, I think."

My grip on Blitz's hand is like a lifeline. "The aunt met with Dad privately, and then left Denham with us."

"Your mother let that happen?" Blitz asks.

"She wasn't happy about it, but Dad said he was homeless, that he was a distant cousin's kid. We only had to have him two years, until he graduated."

"Was he an all-right kid?"

Remembering Denham the way he was then softens me. I can breathe again. "He was larger than life. Wild, for sure. He came in with his big black boots and silver chains and a tattoo even though he was underage. But he was a charmer, you know?" I realize I'm gushing a little and add, "Even though he'd been kicked out of two schools."

"So obviously something happened between the two of you."

My body goes cold. I can't talk about that with Blitz. They are my most private memories.

I decide to keep it simple. "Yes. It went on for a couple months and then one day Denham just couldn't take it anymore. He told me my dad was his father too."

"God," Blitz says. "I can't even imagine what that felt like."

"I ran straight to them. Dad exploded and kicked Denham out. He drove him back to the aunt's. I didn't see him again."

"So you didn't know you were pregnant then?"

"Not for another several weeks. I was upset, not eating, pretty distraught. Anything that would have been a pregnancy symptom was just mixed up in my distress."

"And then you moved."

"Dad brought us here so no one would know about the baby. He was so shamed. So angry. No one would talk to me. I was hidden from everyone."

Blitz leans over the center console and takes me in his arms. "That must have been incredibly lonely."

I shake my head against his shoulder. "But it wasn't. I wasn't alone, you know? I had the baby with me. I could feel her moving. It was like a miracle. I would talk to her and sing."

"Then you gave her up."

I pull away just enough to look into Blitz's face. "I did *not* want to. But I had no choice. My parents just did it. I had no way to take care of her. I didn't know anything. If I could do it all over again, I would have refused. Run away. Found a shelter. At least tried. But I didn't then. I was too scared."

"I told you, I can call my lawyer. You were underage. Coerced."

"No," I say. "I could never do that to Gwen. She already lost her husband. I couldn't take Gabriella from her."

He holds on to me again and we sit listening to the wind howl outside the car. I can still hear Denham's shout, "WHERE IS OUR BABY?"

And fear slices through me.

"Do you think he can find Gabriella?" I ask. "He didn't sign anything giving her up."

"Who did you list as the father?" Blitz asks. "On the birth certificate."

"My father wrote down a name. I think he made it up. It wasn't Denham."

"Then we're okay for now," Blitz says, but he looks behind us, out the back window to the front of Dreamcatcher Dance Academy.

I know what he's thinking.

All he has to do is see Gabriella, and he'll know. We've led him right to her.

# Chapter Five

When we get to the hotel, I stand in the shower spray for a long, long time. I have to get ready for this dinner with Blitz's parents, but I'm totally knotted up over Denham.

I remember the day he arrived. Mom and Dad obviously knew about it ahead of time, as they weren't caught off guard when the car pulled up in front of our house in Houston.

It was the summer before I would start high school, and life was still pretty normal for us. My friends from middle school were like me, giggly and obsessed with boys and fingernail polish and whether or not our mothers would ever let us wear makeup.

I knew all the singers on the new show *The Voice* and had a super-serious crush on Adam Levine. If he was behind a singer, so was I.

Then came that knock at the door. I remember sitting in Dad's ratty navy blue recliner, pretending to read the book on my summer list for freshman English class.

The woman came in first. They introduced her as Aunt Didi, but I had certainly never met her and she wasn't a sister of either Mom or Dad. She looked to be in a lot of pain, walking with a cane and taking small mincing steps in her creased old-lady shoes. Her white hair was thin and lay flat against her head.

My little brother Andy was only three and seemed scared of her, hiding behind Mom's leg. Mom seemed to be taking a lot of deep breaths as the woman came in, and had on her biggest, fakest smile.

Then came Denham.

He looked like a young rock god. His jeans were ripped, and he had on a black jacket over a charcoal shirt, even though it was ninety degrees.

He had his hair gelled so it shot off to one side, like he'd just flipped it. He saw me and lifted his eyebrows, then shook his head and looked away, like I was something he shouldn't gawk at.

We were introduced and Aunt Didi stayed around for dinner. Then she left, leaving a beat-up suitcase and a couple duffel bags on the porch. I was shocked but Dad just said Denham had no place to live and would be crashing with us for a while.

Dad didn't seem to know quite what to do with this rebellious-looking teen. He slept in Andy's room on a mattress on the floor. Andy was instantly starstruck and could be found most mornings curled up next to the mattress. The two bonded pretty fast, and it's probably the way Denham treated Andy that made me like him.

Because otherwise, he was kind of a jerk.

Our first conversation came on his second day. Dad was at work. Mom was inside with Andy. She had me outside pulling weeds around the rosebushes. Denham stepped out the back door and lit up a cigarette.

"You can't do that," I told him. "Dad will kill you."

Denham shrugged and blew smoke my direction. "He ain't exactly here. You gonna narc on me?"

He was wearing the same clothes as yesterday, right down to the charcoal shirt. I'd never met anybody like him.

"How did you end up here?" I asked. "Who are you really?"

"Nobody important," he said. "And I'll probably just run off."

My eyes got wide at that. "Where would you go?"

"I got friends on the East Side," he said. He looked up at the canopy of trees that shaded our backyard and kicked at an old plastic teeter-totter. "Somebody will hook me up with a place to crash."

"Dad won't like that," I said.

He took a step closer to me then, and when his sky blue eyes penetrated mine, I felt a little quivery inside. "You sure worry a lot about what your father thinks."

"Don't you have a dad somewhere? Don't you care what he thinks?"

Denham drew in a long pull on the cigarette, his blue eyes fixed on me. "Been me and my mom all my life," he said. "She died two months ago."

"Oh my God," I said. "I'm sorry."

He shrugged, shoving a hand in his jeans pocket. "She wasn't around all that much. I don't really need nobody."

He blew smoke in the air, and I knew I'd rather not be around when he got caught. But I decided something that day. Denham was going to be part of a family once and for all. And I was going to make it happen.

At the hotel, I turn off the shower, instantly shivering even though the bathroom is warm with steam. How could he be back now? When I'd impulsively gone onstage for the finale of *Dance Blitz*, it hadn't even occurred to me that he would see me. Mom and Dad, maybe, if Mindy saw it and her parents caught her and they called mine. I was fine with that. They can't do anything to me. I'm nineteen.

But Denham? He hadn't even crossed my mind.

I wrap myself in a towel and sit on the cushioned stool in front of the long marble counter. The top of the mirror is fogged, but the bottom is clear. I look at myself, remembering the younger version of me. I had confidence then. But the years in between were laden with self-doubt and shame.

Shame I hadn't needed to feel.

He wasn't my brother at all.

Denham had kept the ruse, calling Dad "Mr. Mason" although Mom had him call her Dot, a shortened form of Dorothy that felt more like a nickname for him to use.

Mom liked Denham, quietly bringing him into the family, keeping the smoking away from her home and encouraging him to come along on outings to movies and dinners, even though he tried to stay behind.

That summer had a record-breaking heat wave, and Mom set up a sprinkler in the backyard for Andy.

One day, my friend Paula and I went to the backyard to get some sun and watch Andy for Mom, who had gone to the store.

I wasn't allowed bikinis, even back then, but I wore a tankini where the top was long enough to meet the bottom. Paula's mom was less strict, so she had a ruffled bikini, but it was still pretty tame.

After fifteen minutes of Andy splashing around, and Paula and me chatting about high school starting in a few weeks, Denham came out on the back porch.

He had wisely shucked the leather jacket, since it was pushing one hundred degrees, and had on a tight white T-shirt and jeans. His eyes roamed over me and Paula as he lit a cigarette.

Paula nudged me and asked, "Who is THAT?"

I wasn't sure what to call him. He wasn't related, not a cousin or anything. "That's Denham," I said. "He's living with us." I leaned in to whisper. "His mom died."

"Oh," Paula said. She flicked her long blond hair behind her shoulder and squeezed her arms together to make it look like she had more cleavage than she did.

Denham noticed, his eyebrow quirking as he blew smoke out over the yard. Then his gaze rested on me lightly, like a caress.

"He's into you," Paula whispered. "It must be pretty crazy, having a hot guy like that living in your own house."

My gaze snapped back to Denham. He wasn't trying to hide his interest. My skin tingled where he looked, along my legs, up my belly, and across my chest.

“Have you kissed him yet?” Paula asked.

I nudged her hard. “No way!” I said.

But as Denham kept staring, his gaze constantly dropping to my thighs, I started feeling like maybe I wanted to.

A tap at the bathroom door startles me.

“You okay in there?” Blitz asks.

I stand up quickly, pushing my wet hair back, and open the door.

Blitz waits outside, holding up two shirts.

“Which says, ‘I’ve brought the crazy hottie who disrupted my TV show home to Mama’?”

This makes me laugh. “Go with the blue,” I say, tapping the chambray one. “Purple makes it seem like you’ve been tamed by a woman already.”

“Ah, but I have!” Blitz says, leaning forward to press a light kiss on my mouth. “How are you doing?”

I open my mouth to say, “Fine,” but the words freeze. I’m not fine. I’m terrified.

Blitz sees it. He hangs the two shirts on a hook over the door and leads me by the elbow into the bedroom. He picks up a white robe on the way and wraps it around my shoulders.

“Come here,” he says, settling on a bench at the

end of the bed. He pulls me down close to him, his arms around me. "Tell Dr. Blitz all about it."

I laugh again. Blitz is good for serious situations. Of course he is. He entertained millions of viewers every week for two seasons.

My head rests on his shoulder. "I didn't think I'd ever see him again," I say. "Do you think he'll go after Gabriella?"

"He might," Blitz says. "But judging by his broken-down truck, my lawyers probably charge more than his lawyers."

I sigh. "But what's the right thing to do?"

He squeezes me. "I guess it goes back to what happened back then. You want to talk about it?"

I close my eyes to the beautiful hotel room, the luxury around me, and the sight of Blitz, who has been completely understanding of every step of my withdrawal of my family.

"It's complicated," I say. "All the shame for all those years. Being hidden away like a monster. Having my baby taken away. All for nothing. He was just some kid. His aunt must have convinced my dad he was his."

"Obviously your dad was playing around," Blitz says. "It had to be a credible threat."

That is true. For the first time, I have the moral high ground over my father.

"Denham was almost two years older than me. If you add in nine months for the pregnancy, Dad would have been with that woman early in his relationship with Mom. They weren't married yet."

"But she could do the math," Blitz says. "And your dad must have been pretty anxious to make his own son keep quiet in order to live there."

"Not-son," I correct. What a relief it is to say that.

"I guess he did do right by you in tracking you down to tell you that," Blitz says, kissing the top of my head. "I suppose I shouldn't have knocked him unconscious."

"You were defending my honor," I say. "Again." I remember his flattening a guy on our very first date, a man who insulted me outside a Mexican restaurant.

"Is this too much? You want to cancel the dinner tonight?" Blitz asks.

"No, no," I say. "I've already waited a month to meet them."

Blitz gives me one more squeeze and stands. "We'll get past this, Livia. That guy will be nothing more than a blip in our very long lives."

I head back to the bathroom to get ready for dinner. I want Blitz to be right. But I knew Denham very well. And I can still hear his threat.

*I'm going to find that baby.*

## Chapter Six

Blitz's parents live in a modest house just outside Alamo Heights. When he pulls his red Ferrari into the drive, a middle-aged couple comes out on the porch, which is still decked with Christmas lights since they just got back in town.

I've never done this before, met anyone's parents. I've barely met anyone at all since I was fifteen, just a few people from our tiny church and the dance instructors at Dreamcatcher Academy. I arrange the skirt of my new dress and fuss over the collar of my coat. Blitz comes around to open my door and peeks his head in.

"Remember, if they howl the cry of my pack, howl with them or they will attack you as an enemy."

"Blitz!"

He steps back, laughing, as I get out of the car.

He pulls me into his arms once I'm out and whispers close to my ear, "Just remember, my dad is pretty rough around the edges. Hopefully Mom will make up for him."

My fingers clutch his sweater as I try to steady my nerves. "I'll be fine," I tell him.

Blitz's mother looks friendly as we approach. She wears black dress pants and a shimmery tunic. Her hair is deep black and twisted in a simple bun. She's not flashy, just small earrings and only a bit of makeup.

His father seems to have a natural scowl, his big eyebrows turned down. He wears khaki pants and a deep blue short-sleeved button-down shirt that I know from Blitz is called a guayabera. He's oblivious to the chill. He seems considerably older than the mom, his gray hair thin and combed over.

The house itself is simple, sandy brick with slender white columns on the porch, a single-car garage at one end.

Blitz takes my hand as we reach the steps. "Mamá, Papá, this is Livia. I think you saw her on the show a few weeks ago. Livia, this is David and Renata."

His father snorts, but his mother holds out her arms. "What a brave young girl you are," she says, stepping forward to pull me into an embrace. "You must have been terrified going in front of all those people! Benjamin tells me you are a ballerina."

The father snorts again.

"Yes," I say as she releases me. "Well, I dance ballet. I'm still a student."

This makes the father raise his eyebrows. "Are you in high school?"

"No, Papá, I did not rob any cradle," Blitz says. He seems annoyed by his father's suggestion. "She is at a dance academy."

"Let's go inside," his mother says. "Before this foolish old man in his short sleeves freezes right to death."

"This cold is nothing," his father says. "You are all just too soft."

Wow. This is going to be interesting. I'm starting to see what Blitz is talking about with his father. I take a few deep breaths, prepared for a tough evening with him.

We head inside the house. It's warm, and I take off my coat immediately before I break out in a sweat from the anxiety. Blitz takes it from me.

"I'll get some tea," Renata says and disappears down the hall.

David stretches out in a big brown chair like he's going to act any way he wants, no matter the company. Blitz pulls me next to him on a flowered sofa.

There's a fire burning in a small brick hearth near us. "How was Colorado?" Blitz asks.

"Snowy," David says. "Your mother drags me there every damn year." He picks up a large glass of iced tea from the table by his chair and takes a drink. "I live in San Antonio to stay away from all that mess."

I have no idea what to say. I concentrate on Blitz's hand. He's taken mine and bends each finger one at a time as if he, too, is trying to manage his discomfort.

David has just picked up the TV remote when Renata comes back in with a silver tray of mugs.

"David, we have company!" she says.

He makes a big point of sighing and dropping the remote back on the table.

I glance over at Blitz. He is more or less relaxed, the only hint of annoyance in the tightness of his jaw. I wonder if meeting parents is always this difficult or if Blitz's father is just a hard case. Then I imagine Blitz meeting *my* father, and figure, yes, it's probably always this rough.

I take a mug from Renata and thank her for it, the first words I've said since we sat down.

"I saw the finale, of course," Renata says as she settles on a tall cushioned chair. "I'm glad Blitz didn't end up with that Giselle woman."

"I liked her," David says. "That girl had spunk."

I grip my mug with tense fingers.

"Of course you liked her," Blitz says. "She was a tramp."

"Benjamin!" his mother says. "Be respectful of ladies."

"That tramp was no lady," his father says.

My head is spinning. The family banter tells me a lot about who influenced Blitz the most. I think he was right when he said every nasty thing that got him in trouble on the show came from his father.

"Tell me how you two met," Renata says. "Was it at your dance school?"

Blitz nudges me. "You tell it, Livia."

My hands are shaking around the mug, so I set it down. "Well, I was dancing and there aren't a lot of male instructors there."

David harrumphs. "See, I told you real men don't go to dance school."

"David," Renata admonishes.

I lace my fingers together, remembering I had enough courage to walk on a live television broadcast, so I could surely tell a grumpy father a story.

"So I was surprised to see Blitz, of course," I say. "I didn't know who he was."

"Really?" Renata asks. "I thought everybody knew Blitz."

"I don't watch a lot of television," I say. "I'd never seen the show."

"Interesting," Renata says. "Are you more of a reader?"

"I spent most of my time studying for the SAT," I say.

"Are you going to college?" she asks.

"Soon. I still have to take the essay portion." I'm not sure if I should keep talking about this or go back to the story. I hesitate, looking over at Blitz.

"Tell her how you taught me to *arabesque*," Blitz says.

"Blitz doesn't know a lot of ballet," I say. "So I taught him a few things. The *arabesque*. *Grand jeté*."

"And the five ballet positions," Blitz adds.

"So you got to know each other during these lessons?" Renata asks. "How romantic." She takes a sip from her mug. "So how did Livia end up as a surprise guest on your show?"

"The man who built the academy where I attend took me on a plane to California," I say. I'm not sure how much to say. I can't tell her Blitz was planning to sabotage himself. "He is a producer on the show and felt it would make for really good ratings."

Blitz draws me closer to him. "She's being nice. I was about to screw up everything and she saved me."

Renata looks at him curiously, and is about to ask

more when a timer goes off in another room. "That's the casserole!" she says, hopping up. "Dinner will be ready soon."

She's going to leave us alone with Blitz's father again. David already has his eyes back on the TV remote.

I make a move, jumping to my feet. "I'd like to help," I say.

"Oh, I'm fine," Renata says.

"I'd love to learn from you," I say.

She hesitates. "Well, okay."

"Good," David says. "Let the women get the meal." He clicks on the television.

I glance back at Blitz as his mother and I head down the hall. He's shaking his head and gives me a wink.

## Chapter Seven

Renata's kitchen is warm, organized, and bright, all cream with red accents. Piles of chopped tomatoes, yellow peppers, and jalapeños sit brightly on a counter.

"It smells wonderful in here," I say.

Renata opens the oven and peers inside. "Do you cook much?"

"Yes," I say. "But not Mexican food." I glance over at the tortilla warmer and a pair of uncut jalapeños. "My dad is very much a meat and potatoes man."

Renata laughs. "I'll teach you to make *carne guisada* and *papas pablanos*. That will make any man happy with his meat and potatoes."

"I'd like that," I say. "What was Blitz's — Benjamin's favorite food as a kid?"

"Macaroni and cheese!" Renata says. She slides on

a pot holder and pulls the steaming casserole from the oven. "From the box! I swear every time he went to a friend's house he came back with worse ideas for food."

"But you made it for him?"

She sets the casserole on a wide iron trivet on the counter. "I did. He and his brother Dante wanted to eat like their friends' families." Renata waves her arms toward the window and the street out front. "It's where we chose to live."

"But it's San Antonio," I say. "Lots of Hispanic families live here."

"Yes," she says. "But the neighborhoods are all different. I probably would have chosen something else, but David insisted. Of course, all the things Benjamin was exposed to here were what led him to be a dancer. So, it was good in the end."

Renata scoops up the piles of cut vegetables and peppers and drops them into a large wooden bowl. "Are you from San Antonio?"

"Houston, actually," I say. "We moved here when I was fifteen."

"How long ago was that?" She gives me a side eye as she mixes lettuce into the bowl and slowly adds dressing.

She's trying to figure out my age. "Four years ago," I say. "Coming up on five."

She nods. "Have you met Dante yet?"

"No," I say. I knew Blitz has a younger brother because he called him Christmas Day, but he hasn't made any sort of appearance.

"Ah, soon I will get both my boys together. Dante is like Benjamin, eager to be out and live wild." She smiles at me. "But maybe you tamed the beast."

She passes me the bowl. "Take this to the dining table, if you don't mind. Out that way." She gestures to a second door.

I head there. I'm surprised to see Blitz and his father sitting already. David is in the process of opening several bottles of beer.

"We moved on to the *aperitif*," Blitz says, picking up the bottle. He holds one out to me.

I set down the salad bowl and take the beer. I'm still underage, but I've gotten used to drinking lightly when it fits the situation. In the past month, Blitz has had meetings at restaurants and sometimes at bars, and I prefer to blend in.

I know that the comment about the *aperitif* is meant to be a slight against his father, as I've only heard that word at fancy restaurants and brown bottles of beer wouldn't qualify. The tension between them is pretty intense.

David takes a slug from the bottle and watches for me to sip from mine. We don't drink beer often so I'm not used to it. It's dark and bitter and fills my mouth with an overwhelming amount of flavor.

I try to control my expression, but David lets out a sharp laugh. "You brought home a real young one," he says. "I guess you can teach her to be anything you want."

Blitz brings the bottle down on the table with a thunk. "Be nice to her, Papá," Blitz says. "I didn't bring her here to be abused."

"Bah," David says. "You obviously fancy this one. She's all right. But she's such a skinny mite. How is she going to give birth to my grandchildren with those tiny hips?"

This makes my face flame. *I've already had a baby*, I want to tell him. But of course I can't say that. I set my own bottle down, poorly, and it almost topples. I catch it, my hands shaking again.

"Where's the bathroom?" I ask.

Blitz looks ready to explode, his face red. But he realizes my tactical retreat is better than a standoff. "I'll show you," he says, abandoning the beer and his father.

Blitz wraps his arm around my waist to walk me out of the room. I feel better, having him stand by me. I want to be strong, to yell back at this boorish man. But he's part of Blitz's family. My father would be no better. It's what we endure.

We go down a carpeted hall and Blitz turns me into a door.

The bathroom is long and narrow with a curtained shower at the end.

Blitz comes in with me and closes the door. He draws me into his arms. "I'm sorry, Livia," he says. "He's being worse than I imagined. Or maybe I just forgot."

I rest my cheek on his chest. "I'm okay," I say. "I just needed a moment after the baby comment."

"I know. But he doesn't know. He won't ever know about that."

Is that true? Denham knows now. And he's someone we can't control. He could tell anyone, sell his story to the tabloids, even.

God.

"I have to face my past," I say. "Others know now."

"I'm so sorry I said anything about it in front of that guy," Blitz says. "I should have been more careful. It's my fault."

I shake my head. "It's my history. It happened."

"But he didn't know," Blitz says. "If it wasn't for me, he never would have."

I embrace Blitz, my arms around his sturdy body. "I don't blame you," I say. "We didn't expect him."

"I just saw him, and how he affected you," Blitz says. "I lost my head."

I look up at him. "What do you mean, how he affected me?"

"You were so upset. He was so in love with you. It was so obvious. It caught me off guard." He runs his finger down my cheek. "You loved him a lot too, I'm sure."

I can't deny that. Denham had been my everything for a while. But I wasn't going to think about that. Blitz was here. And he is what I want. I've shown the whole world that by walking onto his show.

"I think you have an edge on him on a thing or two," I say. I meet his gaze and press tightly against him.

"Do I?" Blitz says, the lazy smile I love coming across his beautiful mouth.

"You do," I confirm, and press my hand against the back of his head so that he will kiss me.

This is what we need. To regroup, recenter, reconnect. It doesn't matter who is against us. His dad. My parents. The show. Denham. We are strong. We fought to be here.

His lips are tender and calming. The kiss is easy, gentle, and reaffirming. I love this man. He loves me.

We'll get through this evening together. And whatever Denham will try in the coming days.

Blitz increases his pressure, becoming more demanding and urgent. He explores my mouth, his tongue engaging with mine.

After a moment, he breaks away. "I'm not sure I can keep my hands off you if we go on like this," he says.

I reach for his fingers and slip them under my skirt. "Who says you have to?"

That's enough for him. His mouth lands on mine again, pressing in, devouring me. He lifts me onto the bathroom counter. The fake marble is cold on my thighs, but I don't flinch. I want this. The connection. In his home. With his parents waiting by the beer and casserole.

He reaches for my panties and jerks them down. His fingers slip into me and I moan against his mouth. My hips slide down to give him better access.

He grabs one ankle and shifts my foot up onto the counter. Now he can slip more deeply inside. I lean back, reveling in his expert work inside my body. The tension is gathering around his fingers and I focus on him, the pleasure radiating out from his touch.

He bends down, his mouth there now as well, and this sends me into a frenzy. I hold on to his head, mussing his perfect hair, until I feel my muscles contracting around him.

I cover my face to avoid making noise as the orgasm splinters through me. Blitz doesn't ease up the pressure until I've come all the way down, then he rapidly unbuckles his jeans.

"Come here," he softly growls, his hands moving beneath me to move him close.

"Don't forget," I remind him. I've started the pill but it's still a week before we can be careless.

He nods and drags out his wallet to extract a condom.

When he's taken care of that, I lead him inside, then he's got me, burying himself deeply, lifting me to straddle him. I imagine a dance routine that includes this, and figure it's certainly been done. I wonder if Blitz has ever seen such a dance show, but I'm not going to ask him now, as everything is intense. I feel lightheaded as he lifts me away and drives me down, plunging with an intensity of need that permeates most of our encounters.

His guttural groan precedes the pressure as he lets loose inside me. I cling to his head and shoulders, holding on as his body goes tense and gradually relaxes.

He breathes against my neck, holding on tightly. When he finally lets go and sets me back on the counter, he says, "Can we just sneak out the window and blow off the rest of this dinner?"

My mouth forms a smile as I straighten my skirt and hop down to retrieve my panties. "We'll just decide that every time your father gets testy, we'll come back here and make them wait on us again."

"He's totally going to figure out what we're doing," Blitz says as he buttons his jeans.

"Let him," I say. "Maybe he'll decide I'm as much of a tramp as Giselle and like me as much as her."

Blitz takes my hand. "What did I do to deserve you?"

I kiss his knuckles. "Absolutely nothing. So start earning it."

He laughs as he opens the door. "I will endeavor to do exactly that."

## Chapter Eight

On Friday morning, we head to the academy for my own dance class. I only earned my *pointe* shoes a month ago, and I still have a long way to go before I can dance in them for any length of time. This is no time to slack off.

My original toe shoes were sprayed blue to match a costume for my surprise appearance on *Dance Blitz*, but I have several pairs now to match my new leotards. Blitz has spoiled me since I moved into the hotel suite with him.

As so often happens in Texas, the weather took a dramatic turn overnight, the cold replaced with warmth. I can wear my leotard without a jacket, and Blitz is back in the sleeveless dance shirts I remember from our first days together.

He's been taking my ballet class with Betsy,

finally learning all the basics he skipped early in his training due to his father's disapproval. It's fun being there with him, especially now that the other girls are used to him. They've stopped giggling the whole time.

But when we approach the Dreamcatcher Dance Academy, we see something we didn't expect.

Denham's green truck.

"Shit," Blitz says. "We should have known." He stops the car a couple blocks away.

"Do we go on in?" I ask, my voice shaking.

"I can pummel him again," Blitz says.

"No, no," I say. "Isn't he trespassing?"

"Not parked on the street," Blitz says. "He's wised up."

His truck is faced away from us, but Blitz's Ferrari is bright red and easy to spot. All Denham has to do is turn around and he'll see us.

"What do we do?" I ask. I don't want another confrontation, or for Blitz to hit him again. Why can't Denham just go away?

"We call in reinforcements," Blitz says. He presses a button on the dash screen. The sound of a phone dialing fills the car.

"Cushman and Rowe," a female voice says. "How may I help you?"

"Alicia, this is Blitz Craven. Is Jeff around?"

"Hello, Blitz," she says. "Let me see if he's still in a meeting."

The call goes quiet a moment.

"Who is this?" I ask.

"My lawyer," Blitz says.

Alicia comes back on. "If you can hang on just a sec, he'll pick up," she says.

"That's fine," Blitz says. He reaches over and squeezes my hand. "Jeff is good. He'll give us some sound advice."

We wait, watching the green truck ahead of us. I can see the back of Denham's head through his window. He hasn't turned around, but he might notice the car in his rearview mirror eventually. It's so flashy. I wish we had a plain car.

"He'll see us any second," I say.

"I'll get a rental," Blitz says. "Something very plain."

I try to relax against the seat. The truck is pretty far away still. We're a couple blocks back and under a tree. Maybe he won't notice.

"I can back away if you want," Blitz says. "We can park around a corner."

I shake my head. "No, that's okay. I want to see what he does." I'm deathly afraid he'll go into the academy and make a scene.

A deep male voice pipes into the car. "Blitz! To

what new debauchery of yours do I owe this surprise?"

Blitz laughs. "I'm not in trouble again. Yet."

"Only a matter of time," Jeff says. "I'll name my next office building after you."

I glance over at Blitz. They find the oddest things funny.

"So I have a situation. An old flame of Livia's spotted her on the show and now is camping out on the street in front of our dance school. You should know I did try to knock a little sense into him yesterday when he tried to grab her, but he's come back for more of the same."

"So you assaulted him?" I can hear the tapping of keys. I guess Jeff is taking notes.

Blitz laughs again. "We'll call it self-defense. I don't think that part is going to be an issue. But I don't like that he's keeping Livia from dancing. What are our options?"

"We can apply for a restraining order, but unfortunately, that will reveal even more data, plus it becomes public record. Right now I'm guessing the rest of the world doesn't know who Livia is. Just this guy because he already knew her."

"We can't have everyone camping out here," I say quickly. "I won't be able to come at all."

"What else?" Blitz asks.

"Can someone reason with him? Can you keep this out of the public record?" Jeff asks.

Blitz looks over at me.

"He is the outlaw type," I say shakily. "I think he feels like he doesn't have much to lose."

"What's he after?" Jeff asks. "Is he trying to get Livia to see him?"

Blitz frowns and raises his eyebrows at me. "Should we tell him?"

"I'm sitting down," Jeff says. "And Livia, confidentiality is what we are all about here. Nothing we discuss here is ever shared."

I look down at my tightly laced fingers. This is where my shame has brought me. Except, it's not shame anymore. It's just my history.

"I had a baby," I say. "This man's baby. I gave it up for adoption. He never knew about it." I hesitate. "But now he does."

I expect Jeff to be surprised by all this, but his voice is the same steady baritone as he asks, "Is he named on the birth certificate?"

"I don't think so," I say. "I'm pretty sure my father made up the name."

The key taps are fast now. "How old were you?"

I don't want to say it, but I have to. "Fifteen."

"Do you have a copy of the adoption contract?" he asks.

"No, but there is one up at my church."

"Who handled the adoption?" Jeff asks.

"The church. It's Catholic. There is some organization that does the legal stuff."

"Have Blitz send me all the information on the church, and we'll start digging for that contract."

I'm terrified to ask this question, but I do. "Can he get the baby?"

"Not easily," Jeff says. "He has to be able to fight, find a lawyer, get a judge to order a DNA test. That's lots of hoops to jump through and lots of expense. Is the baby in a good home?"

"Yes," I say quickly. "And it would be terrible for her to be taken away. She has no idea who her birth family is."

"I understand," Jeff says. "We'll protect her as best we can. Blitz, while I have you, let's chat about the court date coming up with the production company."

They start talking about something businesslike, as if this life-shattering event for me is just another case in his files.

I stare out the windshield at the green truck, petrified Denham's going to see us and come out. I picture him with a bat, bashing the Ferrari. Why did he have to see me on the show? Why did he have to come?

I want to undo so many things now. The calendar

pages in my mind start to flip, hurtling back in time. If only I'd resisted him.

But there had been no way to do that then.

After the sunbathing moment, I was very aware of Denham watching me. Paula and my friends might have been giggly and silly around him, but when his eyes clashed with mine, I didn't feel like laughing. Something unfurled in me, something dark and intense. I wanted to feel more of it and see where it led.

Even Denham had to give in to the weather at times. Dad insisted he help out a little around the house, and one day the two of them set out in the backyard to replace some rotted fence posts.

Denham began the work in his jeans and boots, but as the day wore on, and the digging and hacking to get the old posts out got to him, he gave in and put on shorts and a sleeveless T-shirt, then eventually got down to just the shorts.

Andy was three and wanted to go watch, but I had to keep him away or he'd get in the path of their swinging axe and shovel. So I sat in the shade with Andy on my lap, getting a front and center view of each rivulet of sweat that flowed down Denham's back and into the waistband of his shorts.

I really didn't know a lot then. Just shy of fifteen, I ran with a quiet crowd who didn't chase boys, at least not with the intent of actually catching them. Most of the boys we knew were immature and silly, popping bra straps and not really trying to get too close to us either.

But high school was coming. My September birthday meant I was a little older than many of my friends from middle school, and it showed. Back then, Mom wasn't super conservative on what I could wear. She thought of me as a little girl still, so I had a lot of little tank tops and sundresses with spaghetti straps even though I filled them out in ways that weren't simply cute anymore.

So I might have been wearing too little, a stretchy tank without a bra. And he kept looking at me between swings of his axe. And every flex of his muscles made something in me ache.

In that backyard with my brother in my lap and my father close by, it felt safe enough to really pay attention to this boy who'd arrived in our home. He was a mystery, and gorgeous, and my empathy was high for him. I wanted him to feel welcome here. I wanted to know him better. I tried to tell myself I wanted to be like a sister, but I wasn't one. And as his muscles worked the shovel, I realized sisterly was not how I was feeling at all.

There was this moment that day that I remember well. And if I really thought about when things changed, it might have been right then. At one point, he turned around and caught me staring at him.

He must have recognized something in my look, because he didn't smile or say anything. He just held my gaze. It seared me, his brooding expression, and it seemed to promise me — we're going to deal with this.

There was nothing tender about that part of it. It was raw and powerful and full of intense yearning. Later that night, when I went to bed, I kept picturing his face, his body, the sweat, his muscled arms. And my body reacted in ways I couldn't explain. But it all promised so much more to come.

"Livia?"

I realize Blitz has been calling my name. I glance at the dash screen. It's back to the radio. The phone call is over.

"Sorry, lost in thought," I say.

"Do you want to try and go in?" he asks, pointing at the academy.

I stare at Denham's truck. That boy who sweated in my backyard and gave me that hungry look is right there, just a couple blocks away. And now he wants Gabriella.

"No," I say. "I can't risk it."

"Do you want to tell Danika what is happening?"

Danika is the owner of Dreamcatcher Academy and a personal friend.

"Not yet. Maybe he'll give up. And we can get a rental and park behind the building."

Blitz nods and we start backing away from the school. "I'd much rather bash in his skull," he says.

"I know," I say. "But we don't want the news involved. Or the police."

Blitz backs onto another street, and we turn toward the hotel. We'll work out there today. No barre or dance floor, but we'll figure out a way to get around Denham. I can't let him derail my life. And I won't let him keep me from Gabriella forever.

## Chapter Nine

It's the weekend, so we don't hear back from Blitz's lawyer about his progress in finding the adoption contract and figuring out Gabriella's legal status with Denham.

On Sunday morning, we sit out on the balcony of the hotel room, and I realize the church is open. I could probably go into the office during the service, when everyone is occupied, and find that adoption contract. I know where the files are.

I also know where they keep the keys. I volunteered there for years.

Blitz sits next to me, his feet propped up on the rail, sunglasses obscuring his face. The weather is still warm, so we're in lightweight track suits, enjoying the January sunshine.

"Can you take me to my old church?" I ask him.

Blitz slides his sunglasses up on his head to peer at me. "You need to confess something? Because that thing you did last night might have been a crime against the Good Book."

I kick his leg so that his foot comes off the rail and lands on the floor with a thud. He laughs and reaches across the glass table between us to take my hand. "You want to see your brother again?" he asks.

We did go there once a few weeks back so I could get a quick hug from Andy. My parents won't let me see him otherwise.

"Actually, I would probably avoid my parents," I say. "I think I can get that adoption contract quickly and spare your lawyer trying to track it down."

"You sure you want to do all that cloak-and-dagger stuff?" Blitz says. "Jeff can get it."

"Yes, but we can do it faster. And I'm terribly curious about what my father put on the birth certificate. I remember there was a name, but not what it was."

Blitz sits up, both feet down. "All right, let's hit it. Should we put on our ninja warrior clothes?"

"I think you're enjoying this a little bit too much," I say.

"You keep my life very interesting, Princess," he says. "I like it."

We head inside. I want to blend in as we walk into

the church, so I switch to a simple skirt and light sweater. Blitz puts on khakis and the purple shirt I rejected before the parent dinner. He hasn't mentioned when we might see his mom and dad again, but I'm guessing it won't be soon.

"Let's get our church on!" he says.

We head down to the lobby. This time, a plain silver Mazda waits for us with the valet.

"Your rental?" I ask.

"Boring as I could get it," he says. "If you like it, I'll buy you one."

"I can't even drive," I tell him. My parents never let me have that freedom.

"Right," he says. "We need to fix that."

We take off down the sunny streets. I try to steady my nerves.

The last time I showed up at church, we waited in the parking lot for my parents to come out. So I didn't see anyone else or revisit the places I once knew. This time, we have to actually go in.

We arrive just as the service begins. A few late-comers hurry across the lot. "Park on the curb," I say.

"Your wish is my command," Blitz says. "I'm just the getaway driver."

His light manner helps calm me. "I'm going in alone," I say. "You might be recognized and attract attention."

"I would never jeopardize the mission," he says with a wink. "I'll just sit here with my best movie mafia look." He smacks the steering wheel. "I knew I should have brought my mustache collection from LA."

"Oh, Blitz," I say.

"What? You don't think I'd look sexy with a mustache?"

I stare out the window. The parking lot is empty now. It's five after the hour. My stomach flutters with nerves.

Which is ridiculous. I know everybody here. But I'm going in to steal something. I don't think I can risk the time it would take to make a copy at the ancient machine behind Irma's desk.

Actually, I have my phone. I can just take a picture of the documents.

"I'm going in," I say. "I'll text you if anything goes wrong."

Blitz grips the steering wheel and hunkers down low. "I'll be ready."

This makes me laugh as I open the door. Blitz helps, always.

One more latecomer parks as I cross the lot, and I feel anxious that it might be someone who knows my family well enough to approach them about seeing me. I don't want anyone to tip Dad off that I am here.

I try to surreptitiously glance at the car as an elderly husband and wife get out. We know them, but not well. I can't think of their names. Should be safe enough.

They will go through the main door to the sanctuary. I'll be going in the side to the office.

I pass Mom's white minivan and run my fingers through the dirt on the side. They are here, of course. They never miss a Sunday.

The couple moves toward the front of the building. I approach the side and take a deep breath. The office should be deserted. If it's not, I'll think of something.

My hand tugs the handle forward. When the door swings open, I peek in. Irma's desk is just inside, her seat vacant. I feel a pang as I look around the room I used to work in every week.

It's empty.

My shoes are silent on the wood floor as I cross the office. The muffled sound of the organ assures me that the service is underway. This should go just fine.

I head straight for the closet at the back of the room where I know the private forms are kept. When I tug on the handle, it doesn't budge. Of course. It's locked. I knew that.

I hurry to Irma's desk and open the drawer

where she keeps the keys. They are there, as always. The ring jingles as I lift it out and hurry back to the door.

I'm familiar with the keys and pull out the correct one on the first try. The closet swings open. There is a tall file cabinet and I try to remember which drawer has the adoption files. It was low, not high. I remember that.

I try the second from the bottom. It's filled with tax forms and payment slips for the employees of the church for the past couple of decades. No adoption records.

I slam it closed and open the bottom one. Here are dozens of individual folders. This is it. I finger through them. They are arranged by year. I choose 2012 and tug it out.

The file is thin but there are still unrelated papers in it. Some funeral records. A couple wills that bequeath things to the church.

Then I see it. Gabriella's adoption contract.

I sit on the floor and tug out my phone. I snap a shot of the top page and open it to the second. There are many pages to this document, and I'm on page four when I hear a quiet "Livia?"

My heart slams as I look up.

It's Irma, the church secretary.

She's holding a little device and I recognize it as

one that lets her know when someone comes in the side door. I've forgotten it exists.

"Hey," I say. I don't try to cover up the papers or hide my phone. She's already seen it.

"What are you doing?" she asks.

I decide the best thing to do is just keep working, get as far as I can. I flip to the back page, the birth certificate, and snap a shot. "This is my paperwork," I say, working backwards now, snapping the next-to-last page. "I need to be able to read it."

"You can't do that," Irma says, bending down for the papers. "These are private church documents."

I get one more shot done before she picks them up. I want to snatch them from her, but I don't. She looks so shocked, her face red beneath her chestnut hair, piled on her head with bits sticking out.

"I need those," I say. "They are about my daughter. And I have a legal situation."

Irma glances down at the pages. "This is about an adoption. It can't be yours..." Her voice falters, probably as she reads the name on the front page. Her hand presses against the front of her pale blue paisley dress. "Oh my word."

"It was my baby," I say. "I was forced to give her up for adoption and this church was part of it, before my parents let me attend services. Before you and I met." I hold out my hand. "Please give me those back."

"You're so young," she says, but she passes me the pages. "I had no idea."

"I was very young then," I say. "And so was her father."

I drop the packet on the desk and find a page I haven't photographed. I've done two more pages, when I hear Irma gasp and a large man's hand covers the words.

I know that hand. I look up.

It's my father.

"It won't do you any good to fight this," he says. "Your baby is a long way from here now."

I jerk the packet from beneath his hand and flip to another page. "I have a lawyer who will advise me on that."

"Is it that rich man? That dancer?" he asks, his voice harsh. "Did you spread your legs for him too?

"Mr. Mason!" Irma gasps. "We are in the house of the Lord!"

"Ray!" My mom is behind him, and behind her, my eight-year-old brother Andy.

"The Lord does not object to the truth!" my father says. "Are you lying with that man?"

I move away from him and calmly flip the page to photograph it. I only have a couple more, I think.

Inside I want to cry out at what my father is saying, but I have to focus. I need the document.

Still, my hand shakes as I hold the phone over the page, trying to get a clean shot where the words are clear.

"It doesn't matter if you get that document," my dad says. "Your baby is in a good home far from here."

I don't know why he keeps saying that. I know exactly where my daughter is. But I'm not going to tell him.

I get the last page photographed, and I pick up the packet. "Thank you," I say to Irma, and pass her the pages. "I'm sorry I snuck in for it." I cut my eyes at my father. "I'm sure you see why."

Irma takes the pages, her eyes full of tears. "I'm so sorry, Livia. I had no idea."

I look behind my mother at Andy. "I miss you, Buddy," I tell him.

He tries to come around her to get to me, but Mom grabs him and holds him back.

"I'll try to find a way to see you," I tell him.

"Like hell you will," my father says. "I won't have you corrupting him too."

I turn to my father. When I lived with him, I always bent to his will, thinking I had so much penance to pay, I would never be free of my guilt. But now I know better.

"Denham isn't my brother," I tell him. "He was DNA-tested. And now he knows about the baby and wants her."

My mother gasps. "How do you know that?"

I turn to her. "He found me. And he's looking for the baby. I'm getting these to protect her." I point to the paper Irma holds. "And to clean up the mess you all made."

"Didi told me he was my son," my father says, his voice less threatening now.

"Well, she lied," I say. "And you fell for it. For someone who wants to talk about my relationships, you sure have a dirty history yourself. How long had you been seeing Mom when you were with that woman?"

My father's hand comes up as if he would slap me, but Irma steps between us. "You will not lay a hand on this child in God's house," she says. Her voice quivers. "Livia, do you need me to walk you to your car?"

"I'm fine," I tell her. "I'm no longer afraid of him." I head for the door. "I've grown up, Father," I say. "And you don't control me."

Despite my confident words, I feel like I might

throw up as I cross the parking lot again. For a moment, I'm confused, as I don't see Blitz's red Ferrari. The I remember the silver car on the curb, and head toward it.

"How did it go?" Blitz asks as I get in.

"I got the pictures," I say. "Now step on it."

Blitz doesn't ask anything else, just punches the gas and we speed away.

# Chapter Ten

On Tuesday, we take the silver car and head to Dreamcatcher. Blitz has had mustaches delivered and wears one stuck to his face as we pull into the parking lot. I'm wearing a big hat and sunglasses.

"I don't think the mustache is necessary," I tell him as we approach the academy.

"I just wanted to look dashing for your ex," he says.

"Oh, Blitz." Despite my anxiety, I have to laugh.

Denham's green truck is still parked on the curb.

"I wonder what he does in there all day," I say.

"Watches *Dance Blitz* with his hand down his pants," Blitz says. "I've heard I'm pretty handsome."

"Blitz!"

We pull into the lot and drive through to the side

of the building. I don't know if the back entrance will be unlocked, but I can call Danika if I need to and ask her to let us in.

Of course, then we'll have to explain why. But it's worth a shot.

Blitz looks at himself in the rearview mirror and smooths his mustache. "I just might grow one myself," he says.

We get out of the car. There's no one near us, and the green truck isn't visible from this far back. We hurry to the metal door near the delivery platform.

Blitz tugs on the handle, and thankfully, it opens. We step into the backstage area still crowded with Christmas recital props.

"I have you in the dark again," Blitz says, pulling me against him. "Will you fall for the exotic mustachioed man?" He turns my face to his and kisses me.

"Ick!" I say, pulling away. "Your fake mustache is prickly!"

Blitz runs his fingers along it. "It's soft as a baby's butt!"

"A baby porcupine, maybe!"

Blitz laughs and pulls it off. "I guess if it's going to get in the way, I don't want it." He tosses it toward an open trash can near the door.

"We need to get to class," I say.

"Slave driver!" Blitz says, but takes my hand and leads me through a side door to the storage room.

I squeeze his fingers as we pass through the racks of costumes. Blitz kissed me for the first time here, and we have a lot of fond memories in this space. I spot the top hat he wore once and smile. Blitz has always made my life easier and more fun. If the public really knew him, they would never have tried to burn him at the stake for one terrible Tweet.

Even though it had been a bad one, an image of a naked show contestant in his bed and a very disparaging message. But Blitz has worked hard to apologize and get his public image repaired. With *Dance Blitz* behind us, we could fade into obscurity if we wanted.

The exit of the storage room comes out at the end of the hall where all the dance studios hold classes. The corridor is bustling with young dancers, mostly preschool children since it's a Tuesday morning.

We head into Studio 3, where Janel teaches the wheelchair ballerinas. I've assisted this class for over a year and lobbied for its existence shortly after Gabriella's accident. It's the first place I got to know my daughter.

And I will not let Denham know about her if I can help it.

Two of the girls have already arrived and are warming up with arm lifts.

Another comes in right after us. Janel asks Blitz to grab the sparkle batons. She's looking for new ideas for the girls to dance with.

I love how he instantly goes to the corner to grab them. He's no diva, despite his incredible popularity and fame from his show. Once again, I feel like the luckiest girl in the world.

Gabriella rolls in, and Gwen waves at us. I wonder if I should warn her about Denham. What if he sees Gabriella in the parking lot and thinks she looks like me? Would he go up to them and ask about her?

But he can't know she's here. He's stalking me, not her. Nobody knows. What is he doing, exactly? Intimidating us, I guess. He thinks we will snap. Maybe once I would have. But with Blitz, I feel strong. I won't give in.

Despite our anxiety and the green truck outside, class goes on as usual. We work on the girls' turns and arm positions. As much as I loved dancing with the Nutcracker music, it's nice to move on to other things now that the recital is past.

Blitz's phone buzzes nonstop during class and he finally shuts it off. I look at him quizzically from the other side of the room where I'm working with one of the girls. He shrugs and shakes his head like it's nothing.

When we've finally escorted all the girls out, including Gabriella, Blitz takes my arm and leads me to a bench in the hall. "I got a bunch of info from the lawyer," he says.

His finger swipes through message after message. "Your sweet boyfriend has built up quite the rap sheet in his meager twenty-one years." He pauses at one of the miniaturized document scans and zooms in. "Three counts of assault, two burglaries, three check frauds. Done some time, about eighteen months. Just dumb luck he saw the show between stints in the slammer."

He scrolls some more. "And this is all just since he started getting tried as an adult. Sounds like he had more as a juvenile that's probably still sealed."

"He was always pretty troubled," I say. "But he didn't do any of that stuff when I knew him."

"Tough life, looks like," Blitz says. "But the lawyer says even if he does find a way to challenge the adoption, which would be a significant expense just in getting a judge to order the DNA test, lover boy would have to do all sorts of service plans to convince anybody he could be a fit father."

"I don't want them to take Gabriella from Gwen." I realize I've said her name out loud and glance around us in a panic. Fortunately, only Aurora's toddler class is running, and the parents tend to sit inside the studio for that. The hall is quiet.

"We will do everything we can to prevent that," Blitz says. "Jeff says we can do all sorts of delays and changes of venue to make hiring a lawyer too expensive for him."

"Did you send him my shots of the adoption papers?" I ask.

"Yes, he's got them."

One of the jazz instructors, Jacob, pops out of Studio 2. "Hey, Blitz, I've got a kid here who's showing some serious potential in contemporary. Can you take a look at his moves and give us some pointers?"

"Sure," Blitz says. "You okay, Livia? You want to come in with us?"

"No," I say. I really want to just sit and think. Dreamcatcher is my happy place. "Maybe I'll dance a bit in an empty room."

"Sounds good." Blitz pops up and heads into the studio.

But I don't go into a room to practice, even though I should. I've only had my *pointe* shoes for a month, and I really need to work.

Instead, I think about Denham. I knew he had a criminal history, but I told Blitz the truth. He was fine when he was with us. But he did tell me about his life before us and the things he'd had to do.

When we had that conversation, nothing had happened between us yet. He'd ogled me in a bathing suit, and I'd obsessed over sweat trickling down his back. We'd had a lot of meals together and recently Mom had taken us both shopping for school supplies.

I found myself wanting to be around Denham all the time. So when Mom took Andy to the park for a playdate, I stayed home in hopes of talking to him.

He stayed put in his room, though, and didn't answer when I knocked.

I gave up. None of my friends were available to come over, so to pass the time, I put on my bathing suit to get some sun.

But looking at myself in the mirror, thinking of Denham watching me, gave me a hot feeling that made me feel more alive than I had ever been. I experimented with the tankini, rolling the top up until it exposed my pale belly. It could use a little color, I reasoned, even though I could picture Denham staring. Another thrill zipped through me.

I picked up a beach towel and a pair of sunglasses and opened the door to my bedroom with as much noise as I could, hoping Denham would come out of his room.

Except he was already out. He was in the kitchen,

pouring water in a glass. He wore shorts, and had been doing so more and more since the day he worked in the yard. He was facing away, so I passed behind him silently and reached for the back doorknob.

When he turned and saw me, his eyes locked on my body. I froze, my hand on the cool metal, trying to stay nonchalant as his gaze traveled along my legs, belly, and rested on the top of my suit. Something happened and I glanced down, seeing my nipples puckered like it was cold, even though it wasn't at all. Without thinking, I pressed my hand to one, and Denham let out a little strangled sound.

When I looked up at him, he had forgotten the glass, and water was overflowing into the sink from the faucet.

"Your glass is full," I said, and he didn't respond for a moment. Then he realized his hand was wet and he reached to shut off the flow.

I managed to open the door. "I'm going outside," I said.

He nodded and brought the glass to his lips. But he forgot how full it was and splashed water on his chin. I laughed a little and headed to the yard.

When I glanced back at the house, I saw he was standing by the window over the sink. My body felt on fire. There was this drumbeat inside me now and I needed him to look at me. I felt desperate for it.

Even as I sat in the chair and adjusted the back so I was angled to the sun, I imagined him sitting next to me, his eyes devouring my skin. Then he wouldn't be able to resist and would lean over, his lips gently kissing mine. It would be the most incredible thing in the world.

Every kiss I'd ever seen in any movie had looked fantastic. There was more, but the steps to sliding into a bed together were fuzzy to me. That didn't matter. If Denham kissing me felt as incredible as I knew it would, that would be enough.

I arranged myself in the sun, leaning back, dropping the sunglasses over my eyes. I couldn't tell anymore if he was watching me, but I imagined that he was, leaning against the kitchen counter, desperately wishing to kiss me.

Then the back door slammed.

He was here.

I kept my eyes closed, as if his arrival wasn't anything I should pay attention to. But as the moments unfolded, I got curious. I opened one eye, and inhaled sharply to see him sitting in the grass near my feet, just inches away.

"Anybody told you how beautiful you are?" Denham said.

"No," I said. "I'm actually sort of awkward. My knees are weird and my hip bones stick out and —"

"Stop it," he said. "You're perfect." He shifted closer, so he was next to my knees. "I can't stop looking at you. Does it bother you?"

My throat got all tight, so I just shook my head no.

"Good," he said. "I won't lay a hand on you. That wouldn't be right, living here and all, but I'm glad you're all right with me looking."

My belly sank. Did this mean he wouldn't kiss me either? I had already imagined us walking down the halls of my new high school, holding hands. The other girls would be all jealous, this cool, confident boy in his jeans and black jacket and chains belonging to me.

But he was right. We lived together. Something about our closeness made the whole thing feel wrong, although I wasn't sure how.

I shut my eyes again, my skin prickly with him so near. I heard him shift on the ground next to me but forced myself not to look.

After a while, the sun got to me, sweat trickling in uncomfortable places. When I turned to look, Denham was still there, his gaze fixed on my legs. He sensed me watching, and his eyes met mine.

I could actually hear the thunder of my heart.

How could we stay so close to each other and not do anything? I was desperate to have him touch me, press his lips against mine. Anything to ease this terrible ache I felt.

My voice shook a little when I asked, "You getting used to being here?"

He kicked back a little, resting on his elbows, facing opposite me in the grass. I stared at the fading restaurant logo on his white T-shirt.

"It's all right. Not looking forward to school starting."

"It's hard to be the new kid, I guess."

He shrugged. "I won't go any more than I want to."

"You'll skip class?"

He turned to his side and plucked a blade of grass, examining it between his fingers. "I do pretty much what I want."

"Won't that keep you from graduating?"

"Don't care. I can make more money selling stolen car parts or doing deliveries for people than anything I'd do with a diploma."

I sucked in a breath. "You steal car parts?"

He laughed. "It's easy. Especially pricy accessories like custom wheels and light runners. There's a whole market for those things."

"You're not afraid of getting caught?"

"I've been caught. My friends bail me out. I act all sorry to my juvie officer. I walk."

I sat up. "You have a juvie officer?" Now I was prickly for different reasons. This boy was a criminal! "Does Dad know?"

"Of course he knows. They contacted him and approved the move." His grin was deadly. "I'm allegedly going all straight now that I have a proper male role model."

I settled back down on the chair. "What is it like to steal something?"

He quirked an eyebrow and my heart sped up again. "It's a rush," he said. "The idea of doing it is a tickle, sort of like this."

He ran the blade of grass along my shin, and I shivered.

"And you want to scratch it, to do something really risky and get away with it." He slid the tendril across my knee. "It's intense, like riding a wave."

The grass moved up my thigh. I was feeling it, for sure, the tiny tender blade sending a prickly charge over my skin, his hand so close I could almost feel it. That heat unfurled in me again, but not in my belly this time. Lower. It was unsettling and strong.

Denham wasn't looking at me now, but at the slender piece of grass making its way along my leg.

This was crazy, the heat, this boy, his closeness, the caress as he skimmed my body.

It moved up my thigh, daringly close to dangerous places. I couldn't breathe, couldn't move. No one had ever acted like this. Not even in movies. Who was this boy?

The gravel crunched on the side of the house. Mom's minivan pulling in. Denham looked up at me, his face devilishly charming. He pulled the blade of grass away. "To be continued," he said.

As he walked back into the house, I yanked my swimsuit top back into place, covering my belly. I wanted to go in, but couldn't yet, rooted to the chair. I closed my eyes and pictured all sorts of things, remembering Denham's words about the rush, riding the wave, the itch that needed a really intense scratch.

And his promise. *To be continued.*

I shake my head to chase away those thoughts. In the hall of Dreamcatcher Dance Academy, a door opens and a mom comes out with a small crying girl in her arms. She holds the little dancer close. "I'm sorry you fell down," the mom says and kisses the girl's knee.

"I got hurted," the girl says between gulping sobs.

"I'm right here," the mom says. "You'll be all right."

I imagine all the hurts Gwen has kissed away for Gabriella in her four years. Then I picture Denham trying to take her away. What would he teach her, exactly? How to jack up a car and steal its tires? How to get parole?

I stand up and head over to Studio 2, where Jacob teaches his class. Blitz is inside, doing a dramatic spin for the kids. They try to follow his example, and Blitz instructs them in how to adjust. He's good. Good with the little girls, the energetic boys.

Good with me.

I turn to head into one of the empty studios. There's always one thing I can do to help me through my anxiety and fear.

Dance.

## Chapter Eleven

Wednesday is our free day. No class to teach. No class to take.

Sometimes Blitz and I work out here at the hotel. Other times we head to Dreamcatcher to practice.

Today we hang out in bed well past our usual time. Blitz holds me close, the sheer silks draped along the frame keeping the outside world away.

I've learned to sleep naked, as that is what Blitz prefers for himself. His skin is heavenly against mine. I feel safe and warm and protected.

He strokes my hair. "What should we do with this day?" he asks.

I turn to him. I'm tired of thinking about our struggles. Denham's green truck parked at the academy. My past. Blitz's future.

"I just want to spend it with you," I say.

His hand pushes my hair back from my forehead. "Every day with you is a miracle," he says.

I feel the same.

His lips meet mine. I've grown comfortable lying next to him. Gone is my shyness or insecurity. It's dim in the room, the hotel's blackout curtains keeping the day away, so I break the kiss to get up and slide the heavy fabric aside.

Light floods in, illuminating the bed.

I turn to Blitz. He's lying there on top of the sheets, his lean dancer's body exposed. I am too, my black hair falling down my back.

"You are gorgeous," he says. "I could lie here and stare at you all day."

"You're quite the picture yourself," I say. I push aside the silks to crawl back onto the pure white bedding.

"You cannot do that," Blitz growls. "I cannot resist you when you come at me that way."

I lean down to nip a little bite near his ribs. "Who says you have to?"

He groans and closes his eyes. He's so erect, so close to me. I bite my way down those abs that make women swoon on his dance show. Then I've got him, tasting him, making him grab the sheets with both hands.

"Jesus, Livia," he says.

I feel hot and needy. My hands make their way up his thighs, taut and strong, dancer's legs. He shudders a little, and I know I'm taking him close to the edge. So I release him and work my way back up his body.

"I'm going to take you so hard," he says, his hands on my waist.

I giggle as he flips me over on my back. My hair is everywhere, and by the time I can move it aside, his face is at my thighs, his fingers spreading me wide.

I suck in a breath, moved by the work he is doing. Now it's my turn to clutch the sheets.

My hips move with him, and his hands slide up to massage my breasts. When I am just about to peak, he drifts away. I can feel his smile as he nips his way up my belly. "Turnabout's fair play," he whispers.

I groan and grasp his head in my hands. "Take me right now, Benjamin Castillo," I say. "Or I'll do a Burn Blitz Burn Tweet that will go so viral, it will make Twitter history."

He laughs. "You have me by the tail, Princess."

"Not yet," I say.

"Oh yeah?" he taunts. "How about this?"

In one swift thrust, he's inside. I gasp and clutch at him. "Blitz," I say, then completely forget what else I had planned to say.

He works me over, his face above mine, his

rhythm fast and hard. "Livia," he says. "You know what I want from you."

I do know. I close my eyes, lost in the sensation. He moves with grace and speed, and my body responds, hungry and eager.

His fingers move between us. My back arches. I can't take it. I need this. I want it. Before I can make another coherent thought, I'm over the top, crying out. Bliss kisses me, moving fast, keeping up, then he holds still.

"What?" I ask him.

"Is it time?" he asks.

I know what he means. The pill. Our safe zone.

"Yes," I tell him. "It's been long enough."

He only has to move a moment more and I feel it, and want to laugh, giddy. The warm rush of him inside me, emptying himself into me. We've never been so free, so close, so able to connect.

He drops his forehead to my shoulder. "God, Livia," he says. "That's...so wild."

I hold on to his shoulders. "I know."

"I actually haven't ever done that."

I go still. "Really?"

"Too...risky."

I think about all his paternity suits. Those poor women. What were they thinking if he hadn't even... wow. It wasn't possible.

"I'm glad," I say. "I get at least one first with you."

He shakes his head against my neck. "Not true. There are others."

I run my fingers through his hair. "What else, then?"

He lifts up and gazes into my eyes. "I haven't told anyone else I loved them," he says.

I scrunch my eyes at him. "Um, season one, episode six," I say. "I believe her name was Rebekka? With two k's."

He groans. "The producers made me," he says. "That doesn't count."

I wrap my arms around his neck. "I believe you," I say. "And I'm glad that I'm the first for both things."

He kisses my forehead. "I know what we should do today," he says.

"More of this?" I ask, gesturing to our bodies.

"Well, yeah," he says. "But I want you more independent. Let's get you driving."

"A car?" I ask.

"Yes," he says. "A car."

I let out a rush of air. "Okay, but I'm not sure San Antonio is ready for me to be behind a wheel."

Blitz laughs. "If the city can handle me, it can handle you."

And that's how, a few hours later, we end up at the huge empty parking lot of the Alamodome.

Blitz sits beside me in the passenger seat in the rented Mazda. I look over all the dials and controls. It's overwhelming.

"It's easy," Blitz says. "Cars today are nothing. They practically drive themselves."

My hands grip the leather circle in front of me. Despite having tons of space all around me, row after empty row, I can't quite bring myself to move. I don't want to embarrass myself in front of Blitz. It's been a really long time since I even thought about trying this.

"So let's go over some basics," Blitz says. "This is the gear shift. D is for drive. R is for reverse. You don't have to worry about all these other ones right now."

"What is N?"

Blitz laughs. "N is for never use that."

My face heats up. "Why shouldn't I use it?"

"It self-destructs."

"Blitz!" I try to move the lever to D but it won't go. "Why doesn't it work?"

"You have to use the Force."

"Blitz!"

"Okay, okay. First put your foot on the brake. It's the wide pedal in the middle."

I try to look down there, but my legs are in the

way. When I lift my foot and spread my knees to try to see, Blitz says, "Now that's a position I like to see in a car."

"Blitz, I'm going to hire some handsome instructor if you don't help me."

He tries to control his laughter and holds up his hands. "Okay. I'll do better. I promise."

I spot the wide pedal and put my foot down on it. It pushes in an eerily cushioned way, like I'm squishing something with it. "That's gross," I say.

"The brake pedal?"

"Never mind. The other one is the gas, right?"

"Yes. It makes you move."

"Okay. Wide one brake, skinny one gas. Should I push them both at once?"

"No, no, always use your right foot for everything. You don't ever want to push them both."

"Or I'll self-destruct?" I toss him a saucy expression.

"Let's go with that," Blitz says. "So put your right foot on the brake, then use your right hand to push in the little button on the side of the gear and move it into drive."

I follow his instructions. But I'm so nervous my foot slips off the brake and I hit the other pedal. We shoot forward.

I jerk my foot back. Now my foot isn't on any pedal, but we're still moving forward.

"I'm not hitting the gas!" I say. "Why are we going?"

Blitz tries to look relaxed but he's clutching his seat belt. "You need to hit the brake now. Gently, though, don't slam it."

I lean down to look for the pedal again.

"Eyes on the road!" Blitz says.

"It's too much to do!" I say. We're still inching across the pavement, aiming for a pole with a parking lot marker at the top.

"You can do it," Blitz says. "Use your foot to feel for it."

I move my foot again and manage to hit the gas, shooting us forward.

"Forget the pedals for a minute," Blitz says. His voice is calmer now. "Just turn the wheel to the right."

I turn it. It is tighter than I thought it would be and moves slowly. I expected it to spin like a bicycle tire. We shift to the side of the pole.

Blitz lets out a sigh. "Let's just do this a moment. Feet off the pedals and turn the wheel so you can get a feel for how the car moves."

We putter around for a while, me moving the wheel one direction or the other. Blitz settles back in his seat.

"Okay, now feel for the pedals but don't push one or the other down. Just find them with your right foot."

I move my foot around. "I have the brake," I say.

"Gently push it down."

I press my foot on it and we glide to a stop.

"I did it!" I say. I lean over to give Blitz a hug, but my foot slips off and we start moving forward again.

This freaks me out so I stomp on the brake. This time we slam to a stop.

"That works too," Blitz says.

"I need a break," I say. "How do I make this thing stop moving?"

"Put the gear in park," he says.

I shift the lever. This time when I take my foot off the brake, we stay still. I let out a sigh. "This is stressful," I say.

"Wait until you get into rush hour traffic," he says.

"Never," I say. "I'll take taxis."

We look out over the empty concrete. The sun is bright and Blitz's face is a frown.

"I know my driving is not what is making you so tense. What's wrong?" I ask.

Blitz stares out his side window, his face turned away. "I'm going to have to go back and forth between LA a few times in the next week or two. I have a meeting about the show, and a court date Jeff thinks I should attend in person."

"Should I go?"

"You can, absolutely," he says. "But you'll miss a lot of wheelchair classes and Gabriella's private lessons."

I frown. I don't want to do that. Plus, I'm trying to get in shape for more *pointe* work in ballet.

"I can't let her down," I say. "We're just getting started."

"I also want you to be more independent," Blitz says. "We should go to the DMV and get your driving permit soon. But I'll leave a car and driver for you to get to dance. I'll make sure he seconds as a bodyguard since your ex is stalking the academy."

"How long will you be gone?" I ask.

"Just one night this time. I'm minimizing everything. But if you go with me, you will miss both a private lesson and your own dance class."

"It's just one night, I guess," I say.

"Our first night apart since you barged on to my show," he says. "I don't like it. Particularly with lover boy around."

"He won't even know I'm there," I say. "We snuck in easily enough yesterday."

"We did. I'd feel better if Danika knew." He takes

my hand off the steering wheel and brings my fingers to his lips.

"It's hard for me to tell her."

"I know."

He holds my hand in both of his. We sit for a while in the sun-warmed car. What would Danika think of me if she knew about Gabriella? She has a lot of power as director of the academy. She could take me out of the class, end the private lesson, insist we tell Gwen that I'm the birth mother. Anything.

I can't do that. Can't risk it.

I pull my hand from Blitz and put the car back into drive. I have to be strong. Brave. Independent. Driving is a good first step. I'll get my license. Be able to get myself around. Maybe I'll confront Denham on my own, without the threat of Blitz making him act crazy.

My foot eases off the brake. This time, instead of just puttering slowly, I carefully press the gas. We don't shoot forward, but gradually accelerate. I circle around one of the poles and head across the lot again, this time trying to follow the lines rather than shooting aimlessly across them.

I haven't told Blitz this, and I don't plan to, but I did have a driving lesson once before. In Texas, you can get your driving permit at age fifteen to prepare you for a license at sixteen. So as my fifteenth birthday approached, Denham took it upon himself to teach me how to drive.

It was several weeks after his arrival, past the sunbathing, the fence work, and the blade of grass up my thigh. We hadn't gotten much time alone. On this night, Mom and Dad were watching television, and Andy was already in bed. School would start in a week.

While we were all sitting in the living room, a commercial came on for some driving school and Dad scoffed at the price.

"When it's time for Livia to learn, I'll teach her myself," he said.

Denham's head popped up. "I already have my license," he said. "I can show her some basics."

"You have to be eighteen, I believe," Mom said from her rocking chair.

"Let the boy show her a few things," Dad said. "Take her over to the high school parking lot." He tossed Denham the keys to his Jeep, the car he had before the Pontiac he drives now.

Denham's eyebrows hit the ceiling. "Really? You'll let me drive it?"

"I don't see why not," Dad said. "You've had your license a while and the school is only a mile away. It can't hurt, right, Dorothy?"

Mom's lips were pressed tight, but she nodded.

"The boy can be useful!" Dad added. He was clearly chuffed that his decision to take in Denham could benefit the family.

So Denham and I headed out the door. The days were still long, so it wasn't even dark. We jumped into the Jeep and Denham cranked it up.

He talked me through the mechanics of driving as we rumbled down the road to the high school. My body fairly bounced with excitement. I was alone with Denham, about to drive for the first time, and at the high school too!

We pulled into the large lot, and Denham dropped the car into park and got out so we could switch places. As we passed each other at the back, he grabbed my arm. "You nervous?" he asked.

"A little," I said.

His eyes caught mine and I felt that tickle again, like the sliver of grass on my skin. The rush he talked about when stealing. He was my wave to ride.

I got behind the wheel, scooting forward so I could reach the pedals. Before Denham could even buckle, I'd moved the gear and pressed the gas.

"Whoa!" Denham said as he was knocked against the back of the seat. "Now that's what I call driving!"

We circled the lot, me alternately stomping the gas or slamming the brakes, until I felt I had whiplash. Denham encouraged the craziest moves, whooping and shouting for me to aim for the front doors and floor it.

When I finally put the car back in park, my throat was hoarse from laughing. I got out of the car so we could switch places again.

This time when we crossed paths, Denham clasped my waist, lifting me up and spinning me in a circle. The rush passed over me, no longer a tickle, but a wave, just like he said.

He lowered me slowly, my body sliding down his. When my face reached his, he leaned forward, and it happened. His lips met mine.

The kiss was lingering, careful, and quiet, the opposite of how we'd been in the car. I felt aglow.

When he let me go, I was warm with his attention, calm and happy.

"I shouldn't do that," he said, taking a step back.

"Why?" I asked. There was a promise in that kiss, a feeling that there was so much more. I wanted it all.

"I just shouldn't," he said. He ducked away and headed back to the driver's seat.

I climbed into my side, refusing to look at him. I understood what he meant. We lived together. It wasn't right.

But that didn't stop me from wanting it.

Back in the rental car at the Alamodome with Blitz, I press my foot on the brake, gliding us to a stop. I'm not driving anything like I did that night with Denham. But I can't compare the two experiences, and I will never speak of it.

There are some things that a woman keeps to herself, I realize. And my first lesson and my first kiss are things that need to be left in the past.

## Chapter Twelve

Blitz leaves early the next morning for his flight to LA. I wander the hotel suite, wringing my hands with anxiety, until I pack for the private lesson with Gabriella.

It's actually the first time I'll have ever been alone with my own daughter. And Denham will be outside the building.

Maybe I should have canceled.

But it's too late now, and I don't have Gwen's number anyway.

So a half hour ahead of time, I call the concierge like Blitz instructed and tell them I'm ready to go to the academy.

Downstairs, a driver in a plain slate blue SUV waits with my name in the window. The doorman opens the back door, but I shake my head. It's too obvious when someone sits in the backseat that it isn't a normal situation.

"Front, please," I say.

The doorman obeys and opens the passenger door.

"Hello," the driver says. His tone is abrupt. He looks like a football player, broad shouldered and wide necked. His blond hair is smashed beneath a jaunty hat.

"Can I take the sign out of the window?" I ask. "We're trying to avoid being spotted."

"Sure." His nod is curt. "You'll know the car from now on."

"And can you lose the hat? I don't want to be obvious."

The man laughs and tugs off the hat, tossing it in the back. "I hate that thing anyway."

"Good," I say. "Thank you." I pull down the paper from the window as we head toward Dreamcatcher. My heart hammers. I definitely want to avoid Denham seeing me when I go in. But I have every intention of deliberately talking to him when I come out.

When we reach the academy, we pass the green truck with Denham inside, and I instruct the driver to take me around to the back. I have my phone in my hand in case the backstage door is locked this time, but just like earlier this week, it opens easily.

I pass through the storage area and into the hallway. It almost feels strange to do this without Blitz. He's been such a constant by my side since December.

Gwen and Gabriella haven't arrived yet. I head into Studio 3 to wait.

I run through some warm-ups, thinking about Denham sitting in his truck just outside. I try to decide exactly what to say to him to convince him to leave.

He was a complicated boy, even at sixteen. He has to know his criminal background isn't going to look good for trying to get Gabriella. He must think of her as a baby still. What would he do with a four-year-old girl in a wheelchair anyway? Surely I can convince him to move on.

The door opens and Gabriella rolls in.

"Where's Benjamin?" she asks. She's in a new emerald green dance leotard with a bright fluffy tutu. She looks like a little queen.

"He had to go away for a couple days," I say. "He'll be back next week."

She looks disappointed, and I try to stuff down

any feelings about that. I'm just the plain old regular dance helper. Blitz is a superstar.

"Why don't we just have fun today?" I suggest. "And make up a little dance we can surprise him with?"

"Yes!" she says, her eyes sparkly now. "We can call it Benjamin's Dance."

"Perfect," I say, waving to Gwen as she heads back out to the hall. "What sort of music should we use?"

We spend our hour listening to songs and coming up with silly dance moves to make Blitz laugh. We practice them over and over until Gwen comes in to remind us it's time to go.

"See you next week!" Gabriella says, lifting her arms for a hug.

I lean down to her, swamped with emotion as I always am when I have to let her go. It's been a good hour. I couldn't bear to lose this time with her. I won't let Denham take it from me.

As they head out and I change to street shoes, I try to muster my courage. I'm going to let them get out of the building, into their car, and out of the parking lot before I go out front to confront Denham.

I take my time in the halls, pausing to watch Aurora with her toddler class, then to chat a moment with Suze at the front desk. She asks about Blitz and I explain he's in LA. When I'm sure Gwen is long gone, I take a deep breath and push out the front door of the academy.

The bodyguard in the SUV should still be parked at the back. There's nobody to get in my way. The wind lifts my dance skirt as I head across the lot. I should have brought something substantial to put over my outfit for this meeting. It's still warm, so I'll be heading to Denham in just a leotard and a sheer skirt.

But it's too late to do anything about it now.

I know when he sees me. He's tapping on the steering wheel, obviously listening to something on his headphones, when he goes still.

His face locks on mine. As I approach the truck, I see the windows are down and his eyes take in every detail of my body in the tight, thin spandex. I stop a couple feet away from the door.

"About time you came to talk to me," he says.

"You going to spend your whole life sitting on this curb?" I ask.

"Don't got much else to do." He leans over and opens the passenger door, pushing it wide with a shove. "Come on in."

I hesitate. I can't have him roaring off with me locked inside.

"I'll stay out here."

"I'm not going to bite," he says. "Although I'll admit you look damn delicious. But I don't have enough gas to get me very far, so you're pretty safe."

I glance around. If I stay out here, I'll be spotted by someone eventually. Suze might ask questions. Or Danika. I wouldn't know how to explain this. And God help me if anyone took a picture and uploaded it somewhere. Blitz would go ballistic.

So I step up and sit on the torn-up cushion and close the door. But I keep my fingers wrapped around the handle.

"You look good, Livia," Denham says. His voice is more casual now, without the drawl and the leer in it.

"Thank you," I say. "So how did you figure out where I was?"

"Googled the hell out of your man," he says. "Wasn't easy to link it all up."

*That's good*, I think. I wouldn't want a million crazed fans here if they knew Blitz was back after the promo video he did with the wheelchair ballerinas a couple months ago.

"We were careful to leave this academy out of the interviews," I say. "How did you find it?"

"When I saw y'all onscreen, I figured you hadn't been together long. Saw he'd been in San Antonio and followed his trail on Twitter and those sleazy celebrity sites. When you got up on those ballet toes, I figured he met you here."

"He did," I say. No use denying that.

"You been an item long?" He breaks his gaze on me for that question, staring out the front windshield. His earbuds are piled in his lap now, white cords on faded blue jeans. He still has the black leather jacket on.

"A few months," I say, stretching it a bit.

He doesn't have the young rebel attitude anymore. His face is more filled out, still handsome, but not the lean, spare look he had as a teen. He's rough around the edges, his whiskers grown out more than Blitz lets his get, and lighter colored. He looks hard, like he's seen a lot. He's been in jail, I remember.

"He doing all right by you?" he asks. His hand drapes over the steering wheel like he's feeling laid back, but I can see the tension in his jaw.

I know this face, I realize. At one time, I knew what he was thinking just by the expression he was trying to hide. Watching him now sends a million memories flooding back to me.

"He is," I say. "Although he's worried about this. About you. What do you want, Denham?"

He turns to me then, his light eyes piercing me. "I

came here to tell you about the DNA." He sniffs. "But now I need to know about my baby."

I don't know what I should tell him. I could lie, say it is a boy and he lives in Nebraska. I could say he died when he was three. I could say I don't know anything, that I hadn't even seen the baby or found out the gender.

But I'm not good at those things. I think the less I say, the better.

"I hired a lawyer," I say. Maybe I can intimidate him into leaving. "I know you have a criminal record. You won't be able to get her."

"So she's a girl," he says. "Imagine that. A baby girl." He turns back to the windshield. "Is she as pretty as you?"

This is why I shouldn't talk. Heat rises in me that I've even said that much. "I don't have her, Denham. She was adopted at birth. It was all legal and square. It's a good family. Please don't mess up her life."

He taps his thumb on the steering wheel. "I don't see how it could be all legal and square if I didn't sign anything. And I might have a past." He glances at me. "But I do know one thing about the courts." He flashes me a smile. "They love reforming bad guys."

My blood chills. "Denham, this is not about you. It's about her. Leave her be. I wasn't happy to let her go either. I was too young to make that decision. But I stand by what's happened, for her sake."

This is the wrong thing to say. I know it immediately. Denham's face lights up and he takes my hand. I want to pull away, but he's got me.

"Livia! Then let's do this for us. Let's get our baby back. We can raise her. You got your man. And that's all right. But let's get her. Let's right this wrong."

I jerk hard to get my hand away. "That's selfish!" I say. "It's not what she would want. She thinks of her parents as her parents!" I must be careful not to say the father has died. This will only fuel Denham's determination.

"She's a kid. She'll recover. When she gets older, she might be mad that she never got to meet us."

I know Denham is right about this part, but there has to be a way in the middle, where Gwen keeps Gabriella and nobody is upset or destroyed by this.

But I remember what Blitz said. Make him fight and keep it expensive.

"You won't win," I say. "We'll fight you."

"Interesting," Denham says. "Interesting that you want to fight so hard not to see her." He picks up his earbuds and slowly rolls them into a coil. "Unless, of course, just speculating here." He winks at me. "You actually know where she is and get to see her all the time. So you're just keeping my daughter from ME."

I've said too much. Coming here was a huge mistake. I fumble with the handle and throw open the door. I can hear Denham's laughter as I dash across the parking lot and around the building.

I've made things worse.

# Chapter Thirteen

When I get back to the hotel, I want to bury myself under the covers and never come out. I have the whole rest of the day and night without Blitz. We haven't been separated since I left home, so this is actually the first time I've been alone, pretty much ever. I suffered through many years of being homeschooled and watched by my hawk-eyed father. Babysitting my brother. Volunteering. Dancing.

But never alone.

I drop my bag on a chair and head to the balcony, my happy place.

I sit on Blitz's seat instead of mine and look up into the sky. The sun is warm, and for a moment, I can block out all the unhappiness of the past hour.

I remember meeting Blitz, and how we danced

the first time. The moments in the storage closet. His first intense kiss. Ballet lessons. Waltzing. That movie we saw early on and what he did to me in the empty theater.

My body shivers. This is making me miss him more.

I stand up and lean over the balcony rail, looking out over the city. In the distance, the revolving restaurant on the top deck of the Tower of the Americas slowly turns.

Despite my efforts, my mind goes back to Denham. I gave up so information. I never should have gone out there. I've only made him more determined to find Gabriella.

I need company. Somebody who knows my situation and can help. There aren't many, other than Irma up at the church, but I can't exactly ask for her advice.

Then there's Mindy. My best friend.

She wrote me after seeing me on *Dance Blitz*. We had a flurry of conversations then. She tried to come up to me when I went to the church to see Andy, but her parents kept her away. Probably my father convinced them I was a bad influence.

I've been bad about keeping up messages with her since I'm always with Blitz. But I'm not now. I head back into the suite to find my phone. Maybe she can meet me at the park.

I could tell her about the baby. I'm not afraid anymore.

I scoop up the cell and tap out a quick note asking if she can meet today. That I've missed her and have so much fun gossip to share.

But almost as soon as I hit send, my phone beeps.

*Message undeliverable.*

That's weird.

I go out on the balcony to get a better signal and try again.

*Message undeliverable.*

Strange. I'll just call and leave a voice mail. I dial her number and tap my foot on the balcony floor. A brisk wind blows in and sends tendrils of loose hair into my eyes. I push them away. Another cold front, I guess. Texas weather is always unpredictable.

The phone never even rings. It goes straight to a computerized voice that says, "This caller is unavailable at this time. Thank you."

Then hangs up.

What?

Did they take her phone away?

Even if they did, wouldn't it ring? Did her parents deactivate it totally?

I head back inside the suite to pace a circle

around the sofa. Is Mindy in trouble? And if she is, is it because of me?

I glance at the clock. It's a little after noon. Her mom and brother are almost certainly at home, eating lunch with her. They are homeschooled, like I was. That's how we became friends.

There's a chance she might answer her home phone.

I dial it quickly and continue to pace the room as it rings. After a few seconds, I get a message that isn't their voice mail. Again, a computerized voice saying the caller isn't available. And no chance to leave a message. It just hangs up.

Surely they haven't disconnected their home line too.

Then I get it.

They've blocked me. My number can't get through on either line.

I sit down on the sofa. They must really think I'm a threat. Me! Mindy's best friend!

I'm really worried for her now. Did she get any other kind of punishment?

I walk over to the polished wood desk in the corner of the room. There's a phone there, one that they wouldn't know to block. I pick up the receiver and puzzle out how to use it. The instructions say to dial 9, wait for the dial tone, then key in the number.

I do that, typing in Mindy's cell phone first.

She doesn't answer, but I do hear her voice on the message. "Hey, everybody," she says. "I'm losing my phone for a while. Don't leave a message, because I can't get it. Hopefully I'll be back soon. Miss me!"

Despite what she says, I do leave a message.

"Hey, Mindy, it's me. I'm staying at a hotel, but I don't know if I'll still be here when you get this. I'll keep trying you, though. I miss you."

Dang. I could try calling her home number from the hotel, but I'm not sure I'm up for talking to her mother, who would most certainly answer if they are watching her so closely.

She's on Facebook. I'll try that next.

The drawer to the desk glides smoothly on its track and I pull out the iPad Blitz gave me for Christmas. It's been my window to the world, which used to be so small. When I lived at home, my parents didn't allow me to have a phone or computer or even watch television. I had to sneak time online at the church when I could, and that was severely limited.

But now, I can look up anything, talk to anyone.

I power it on and head to Facebook. I have a fake profile there that I created to watch Gwen and Gabriella back before they came to the academy. It's how I knew when the accident happened and that I should start a wheelchair dance class.

I bring it up now. I still haven't started an account under my real name, and given my recent bout of fame on Blitz's show, plus Denham stalking me, it's probably not the right time to do it.

But I could friend-request Mindy with the fake one. Then send her a private message saying it is me. She doesn't know I have the account because it is tied to Gwen. But the profile has fifteen or so random strangers as friends, so it wouldn't be obvious right away why I set it up. I want to save the bombshell about Gabriella for when I see her in person.

Facebook pops up. I'm about to search for Mindy when I see something interesting.

Gwen has added a new picture. It's her, Gabriella, and a man I've never seen on her profile before.

He's tall and handsome and has his arm around Gwen. Gabriella is reaching up from her wheelchair and holding his hand.

Gwen has met someone.

I'm so glad for her. It's been well over a year since her husband died. And Gabriella seems to like him.

I flip through her pictures to see if there are any others, but this is the only one. Then I click to her profile to see if there are any mentions. I find one from a few days earlier.

*I didn't say anything sooner because I didn't want to*

*jinx it, but I've been dating a wonderful man. Gabby seems to love him and I think he's healing both our hearts.*

My breath catches. This is wonderful! I click back to the picture and scan the comments below it. Lots of happy well-wishes.

I roll back the chair and turn to the floor-to-ceiling windows overlooking the city. Gabriella will have a dad again!

Except...her birth father is looking for her.

I stand up and press my fingers to the glass. Denham has a very strong will. He will keep trying. He never gives up.

There was only one time that he faltered in his resolve. And that was in his determination to stay away from me.

After that first kiss behind my father's car, Denham did manage to keep himself out of my way for a while. We only saw each other at dinnertime, and he kept his head down.

He took an interest in my little brother Andy, who was three and had a serious case of hero worship. Andy was delighted that Denham had dropped the brooding act and actually started carrying him around and having wrestling matches. They were always together, playing with action figures or having tickle fights.

Dad was pretty strict, wanting his kids to be quiet

and obey. Denham took on the roughhousing and piggyback rides that Andy had been missing.

I, however, wanted more kisses. I'd felt the thrill of it, and now there was no stopping me. As I tried to orchestrate moments to get Denham alone, I found he always brought Andy along. My little brother became Denham's mini-chaperone.

But it couldn't last forever. Andy's bedtime was way before ours, and it was only a week after that first kiss, the night before high school began, that Mom and Dad headed to the store for last-minute supplies and left Denham and me home alone.

I was determined to figure out a way to wrangle another kiss. I still had this vision of us walking down the halls at school together. Even though I could agree on a thinking level that it wasn't right, not with the two of us living together, my body was driving the cause.

As soon as my parents' car left the driveway, I tried to convince Denham I needed some help organizing my things for the first day of school.

A buzz went through my body just talking to him. I felt driven by the need.

Denham said he wanted to hit the hay early since it was the first day, but his eyes weren't agreeing with his words. Us being alone was having an effect on him too. I knew it. He knew it.

"It's only eight o'clock," I said. "You don't need that much sleep."

We stood in the living room, him near the door as if he needed an escape route. I leaned against the back of the sofa, just a few feet away.

It had been unbearably hot that day, and I wore shorts and a spaghetti-strap tank. Denham had shorts on too, and a plain T-shirt. We were both barefoot and the air-conditioning ruffled his hair, since he was standing right in front of the window unit.

"You have the cool spot," I said, walking up to turn my face to the blast of cold air. "It's insufferably hot in my bedroom. Is it in yours?"

Now we were almost touching, the air cutting a channel between us, my long black hair blowing. I shifted and the tip of my breast brushed against his arm.

He leaped back as if he'd been burned. "Livia," he said. "I have to stay away from you."

I took up his space, turning to fully face the blast of air. I felt like a supermodel on a photo shoot, the wind making my hair fly away from my face, my shirt plastered against my body.

When I looked at Denham again, he was staring at me, his Adam's apple working up and down. Then his eyes met mine, and that was it, everything changed.

He came at me like a bull charging. His hands cupped my head, pulling me to him. This kiss was like an explosion, his mouth opening mine, deep and passionate. It put every movie kiss I'd seen to shame.

My body pressed against his. His hands roamed down my back and cupped my bottom. He pushed me against him and I felt something shift against my belly. He was growing down there, and I could picture it like the drawing from health class, only getting bigger and harder against me.

He wanted me. This was what happened. I wrapped my arms around him and kissed him back with all my might. The world was tilting, like I couldn't figure out where the ground was anymore.

The air blasted one side of us, and Denham moved us away to escape the cold. We walked across the room until we backed against the sofa.

We had separated a bit, but he kept kissing me, now letting his hands run along my sides and ribs.

He was going to touch my body, I just knew it, and I couldn't bear the wait. I wanted him to do it now, to feel what it would be like. His mouth was hot on mine and my jaw ached. I was ready to do anything he wanted.

But then he did something unexpected and thrilling, breaking the kiss and trailing his mouth down my neck and along my shoulder. He slipped a finger beneath the strap of my tank and tugged it aside.

He wasn't really exposing anything new, as thin as that strap was, but it sent a flood of excitement through me. When his lips touched the spot that he'd bared, I thought I'd melt from the heat down below.

Then his other hand came up, just like I wanted, and cupped my breast. My knees felt wobbly and weak. I wasn't sure I could keep standing. His thumb crossed my nipple and the movement created a flash fire through my body. I was addicted, so completely erased by these feelings. I never ever wanted them to stop.

His fingers flirted with the top of my shirt, like he might pull it down and look at me. I wanted him to. I wanted him to see me. I wanted him to kiss me there. My breathing was crazy fast, like I'd run a marathon. Denham seemed controlled and focused.

Out on the street, a car door slammed, and Denham startled. He lifted his head from my shoulder, listening.

I managed to find my voice. "It's just a neighbor. They haven't been gone very long." Please don't stop, I thought. I can't bear it if you stop.

But he did. He pulled back, tugging my strap back into place.

"Shit, Livia," he said. "We can't do this. We can't."

Before I could say anything at all, before I could stop him, he was gone.

~*~*~

I OPEN MY EYES AND LOOK OUT THE HOTEL window. It's painful to compare the boy Denham once was to the grim, hardened man sitting out in front of the academy in his broken-down truck.

I don't know if what we did sent him on that trajectory, or if he was already on it. But once we got started, there was no way to go back.

School started. I didn't get to walk the halls with Denham, and in fact, I rarely saw him there. He was a junior to my freshman, so it made sense. But it still felt like a slight.

The first few mornings, we rode the bus together. But after that, he made friends and hitched rides. I was never invited to go along. As the first week passed, I felt abandoned by him. He avoided me at home more than ever.

School was hard. While I had friends from middle school, our schedules were all different and sitting at lunch wasn't easy, as I scarcely knew the people at my table. Denham had the same lunch period as me, I knew this from stealing a glance in his binder, but I never saw him. I don't know where he went.

I talked very little. Despite being surrounded by people, I felt alone.

One conversation I do remember during lunch, though, was between three girls talking about love. They argued about how you knew if you were in love with someone.

One said it was when you got mad if they talked to another girl.

The second said it was when you couldn't think about anything else.

The third said it was when you knew you wanted to have sex with them.

I sat there listening, and realized all three of those things were how I felt about Denham.

I was in love.

This made me bolder. I felt justified in everything I did. It was love! That weekend, I convinced Mom and Dad to go see a movie and have dinner.

Denham had friends now and protested having to stick around and help me with Andy, but Dad insisted that his obedience was what allowed him to live with us. As soon as they were out the door, Denham stalked to his and Andy's room and slammed the door.

I got Andy fed and ready for bed as early as I

dared and lightly knocked on the door. Denham didn't answer. I was feeling bad about Denham getting stuck there because of my idea, but when I opened the door, that evaporated.

He wasn't there.

"Where's Denum?" Andy asked.

I hurried to the window. It was closed but unlocked.

I could rock his world by latching it, leaving him no way to get in. But I didn't.

"He just went outside for a little while," I said. "Let's read a book."

My mind definitely wasn't on the shark story as I read. I was disappointed and a little angry. He was breaking the rules, assuming I would lie for him.

And why was he so desperate to leave me? We were just kissing. There was no harm in it.

But I did know. My feelings ran strong. My parents wouldn't approve. Denham's ability to live here was at risk.

I should leave him alone too.

By the time Andy was asleep, I felt like crying. I had all this emotion inside and I didn't know what to do with it. I played sappy love songs on my iPod and wandered the house in a miserable daze.

My parents came home, and I said both boys were asleep. Mom popped her head in the room, but I guess she didn't really notice from the doorway that Denham wasn't in the snarl of bedding. Or maybe he actually was home by then. I hadn't been brave enough to check.

I confined myself to my room, my window open a few inches since it faced the backyard, same as Andy's. I might catch him sneaking back in if he was still out. The night was hot, and I had a fan blowing on me, so I almost missed it when he slid his window up.

I leaned out. "Denham," I whispered.

He saw me and turned. "What?"

"Don't wake up Andy. Mom thinks you're in there."

He stumbled back a step, and I realized, he's not all right.

"Are you okay?" I asked.

"I'm fine," he said. "Just a little drunk."

"Drunk!"

"Yeah, you should try it. If you aren't scared." His face was twisted in the moonlight.

My anger flared up. I wasn't the one who was afraid!

"That's rich coming from a boy who's too scared to even kiss me properly."

His eyebrows shot up and he headed my way. "Am I?"

I ducked back through my window. Denham seemed different, really different, with the alcohol. My pulse sped up.

He stuck his leg in my window and stepped in. He glanced at my closed door and down at the fan, which whirred noisily by our feet.

"Is this more of what you were aiming for?" he asked, and snatched me close to him.

His mouth was hot and hard against mine, and he tasted like nothing I recognized, sweet and strong. But it was what I wanted, and I relaxed into it. His hands weren't slow to respond this time. They moved to the bottom of my pajama top and slid beneath to surround my bare waist.

His touch on my skin ignited me. I gasped against his mouth, but he didn't slow down the kiss.

Everything was on fire. I was desperate for him to touch me more, everywhere. I remembered what the girl said at lunch. *You know you're in love when you want to have sex with him.*

And I did. I knew I was young, but all the girls were talking about it. Some of them had already done it, or at least said they had.

His hands moved up and cupped both my breasts at the same time. I wanted to lie down then, to give in, to let him do whatever he wanted.

I found a belt loop on his jeans and tugged him

toward the bed. I could picture myself sprawled across it, my hair everywhere, and him looking at me. I wanted this.

We moved together, his hands roaming my body. I fell back on the bed, and Denham just stood there a moment, looking at me. I could feel him hesitating, breaking away from how he felt and thinking about it too hard.

"We don't have to go all the way," I whispered. "Just show me things. You know things, right?"

He let out a long exhale. The bed shifted as he lay next to me. "We're playing with fire, Livia," he whispered. "Once we go down this path, there's a point of no return."

"We won't go there," I said. "Just close to it. Okay?"

He shook his head. "It's a bad idea, but damn it if I can't resist you at all." He leaned down and planted a gentle kiss on my mouth. "I'm all sobered up now."

"Good," I said. "I want you to remember everything." I hesitated, my heart hammering. "Because I'm in love with you."

His eyes glittered as he searched my face. "Really?"

"Yeah. I think I have been for a while."

His smile was lazy and irresistible. "You're one crazy kid."

I thought I might cry. I wasn't a kid! I would show him that. "Kiss me some more," I said.

Denham watched me, his breath coming fast. I knew it was working. We were beating the obstacles, knocking them down. Nobody knew what we felt. Nobody had to know.

"No way I can resist you," he said. "No way."

And he kissed me again, not just my mouth, not just my skin, but every sensitive place, inside and out. He showed me the things he knew, and I felt like a flower opening its petals to the sun.

We were careful then, not going too far, learning each other, taking no risks.

But he was right. Once we started, there was no going back.

## Chapter Fourteen

I never did write Mindy. The shame came over me again. It didn't matter that I didn't know who Denham was then, or that in the end he wasn't my half-brother. The shadow that darkened those years crossed over me and I couldn't talk to anyone, not even in messages.

I was glad I was alone.

For an hour or so, I distracted myself by poring over Gwen's Facebook page, saving photos of Gabriella to my iPad. Then I felt guilty for stalking her without her knowing and shut it down. My life was a mess. So many lies and half-truths. I thought about this woman who was Denham's mother and the Aunt Didi who dumped him on us. But they were dead.

I wondered if Denham knew his father by now.

That would be Gabriella's grandfather. He might be alive. Another person cheated from knowing her.

I stood up and changed from my dance clothes into sweatpants. The loneliness began to pierce me. I needed to do something useful so I could get my mind off these thoughts of Denham and Gabriella.

But I had loved Denham. And eventually, he had loved me.

That first month of high school was amazing.

We knew our limits. Now that the floodgates were open, Denham and I sneaked around any time we could. After Mom and Dad had gone to bed, he would come to my room, and we would push the envelopes of touching, tasting, and teasing each other.

I wanted more, but Denham was dead set against it. And we were careful not to be seen together too much. There was this glow about us that would be so easy to spot.

Denham quit sneaking out. He still wore boots and leather, but he was softer now, less angry and bitter. He even stopped smoking. Most nights he played with Andy, and he and I stole happy glances at each other from across the room.

One night at dinner, Mom remarked that Denham sure was fitting in well with us.

"I like playing with Andy," Denham said carefully. "He's a great kid."

Andy leaned over in his chair to rest his head on Denham's shoulder. "I love Denum."

My dad grunted, but I could see he was pleased with how it was all working out. Later, I wondered why he hadn't gone ahead and told us that night that Denham was his son. If he had, he could have saved our family so much heartache.

With two seemingly responsible teenagers at home now, Mom and Dad decided to go to San Antonio overnight for their anniversary. I thought about having an entire night to be with Denham, going anywhere we wanted in the house, and felt flushed with anticipation.

We put Andy to bed as usual, and waited a solid hour to make sure he was sound asleep before crashing into each other.

"On the sofa," Denham said. "And the kitchen table."

"Backyard?" I asked. October was still warm in Houston.

"Anywhere you want," he said.

And we did, wearing as little as possible, teasing each other, kissing and touching and doing all the things we'd figured out over the past two months.

When we got into the backyard, Denham

dropped the reclining lawn chair down into the position I used when I would get sun over the summer.

"I want you here," he said. "Like that first time I got a good look at you."

I sat down on it and leaned back. The moon was high and full, casting a light glow over the yard. The neighborhood slept. Our fence was solid and no windows looked in.

"I want you naked out here," he said, and a thrill zipped through me. We rarely undressed all the way, since we were so afraid of getting caught.

But I did what he said, slipping off my clothes in the moonlight.

He did the same, and I saw all of him for the first time. He lay next to me, our bodies pressed tightly together on the lounger.

We didn't speak, just kissing and touching like we always did. The rung of the lounger started to bite into my side, so I shifted onto my back. Denham moved over me, and my heart raced with him in that position.

"I feel so strongly about you, Livia," he said. "What have you done?"

I smiled up at him. "I don't know. Just loved you, I guess."

"I think I get it now," he said. "The love thing."

I thought my heart would absolutely stop beating. "What do you mean?"

"I think I love you too."

Everything soared inside me. I was warm from head to toe. Denham loved me back! There was nothing we couldn't do. We would be together forever.

His body pressed against me at the hips, and I could feel everything, him hard and strong between us. I'd touched him, even tasted him. I knew that part of him well.

But I wanted it the way real couples did it. It was like a molten fire, almost painful in the need. Surely he wanted it too. Especially now that he felt the same as I did.

I kept his gaze as I shifted below him, angling my body so that he was where he needed to be.

He closed his eyes. "Livia," he said softly.

"Don't think," I said.

He eased against me, sliding around. Then he was inside, and my world splintered. The burn was searing at first, then it lessened. But it didn't matter, because Denham was going now, his hands on my shoulders.

I moved with him and found his rhythm. And I understood. This was what made life work. My love for him flooded me and I knew I would never get enough. I would want this and want this and want this.

That first time was risky and unprotected, but had no consequences. It was later that we were stupid. We had condoms that Denham picked up, but they were sometimes in the wrong part of the house, or we'd run out but did things anyway.

We got reckless.

And then we got caught.

I don't want to think on that, alone in this hotel. I push it away and lay on the bed in the room I share with Blitz. I send him a message that I miss him and tuck his pillow under my head. It has been the longest day, but I have gotten through it. Now just a night, and tomorrow he will be back.

I'll return to my happy present, where Denham can't hurt me, and all this will eventually be another terrible dark memory.

## Chapter Fifteen

I wake up at a crazy early hour with a load of missed messages from Blitz.

I filter through the texts and listen to the two voice mails. It's 5 a.m. here in Texas, which means it is only 3 a.m. in California.

His last message was around midnight when he went to bed after a long day of legal meetings and a couple hours at court. One of the contestants of *Dance Blitz* is suing for breach of contract, but he said it was going to work out. Same tactics as we'd use for BD, he said, which is what he's calling Denham now, for baby daddy.

Delay and delay until they can't afford their lawyer anymore. He refuses to settle, at least for now. The suit is ridiculous, just an angry girl who thought she would win.

I turn the ringer back on and head to the shower. My own *pointe* ballet class isn't until the afternoon, but I might as well get the day going. Maybe I can have the driver take me around town. I could go see Irma at church, or drive by the park on the off chance Mom and Andy are there alone. I miss my brother.

I step into the spray, determined to have a better day and not let my past get to me.

Blitz calls late morning and just talking to him lifts my spirits. I tell him a little bit about my run-in with Denham, and that I had spilled that Gabriella is a girl.

"Don't say anything else," Blitz says. "Try to avoid contact. We'll freeze him out on the legal side, don't worry. He'll give up eventually."

"But he's sat outside the academy every day since he got here!" I say.

"We'll talk to Danika together about it," Blitz says. "Maybe we can have a police officer chat him up, make him uncomfortable, even if it's legal for him to sit there."

"But what if she wants to tell Gwen about me?"

"We don't have to mention the baby. Only that he's an ex stalking you."

"Okay."

"I'm heading into the very last meeting with the

producers before I get on a plane," Blitz says. "By tonight, I'll be back to ravishing you."

I laugh a little. "Okay, Blitz. I love you," I say.

"I love you too, Princess. Don't go to dance if you're not up for it."

"I won't."

"See you tonight."

I decide to go for a swim in the indoor pool for some extra exercise that won't tire my feet before ballet. By the time I'm done with that and cleaned up again, it's time for a quick late lunch and to head up to the academy.

The same slate blue SUV and blond driver are waiting for me downstairs. Like before, I get in the front seat.

"I didn't get your name yesterday," I say.

"Ted," he says.

"Do you have to wait here all day for me to call for you?" I ask.

"That's my job." He pulls away from the hotel.

"How much do you know about what's going on?" I ask.

"Only that I'm to drive you anywhere you want and make sure nobody upsets you. But not to follow you inside places unless you ask."

"You'll come inside?"

"You only have to ask."

I wonder if I should do that. But that would be weird and obvious and the dance teachers would talk.

"I'm okay there. I might drive by a park, though. And I might have you walk with me there."

"Works for me."

I don't try to be chatty beyond this. I watch out the window as the world passes by. At least I don't have to worry about Denham spotting Gabriella today. She won't be there.

When we approach Dreamcatcher, Denham's green truck is parked in the same place as yesterday. He said he didn't have much gas for it. I wonder if he's dead broke. How he can just sit there, no job, nothing else to do? I don't know anything about his current life.

But as we drive up, I don't see him sitting in the driver's seat. Is he lying down, maybe? Sleeping? My anxiety grows a little.

Then I spot him. He's walking along the sidewalk. We're about to come up right alongside him!

I frantically dig through my bag for sunglasses, but they aren't there. "How tinted are these windows?" I ask.

"Not as good up here as in the back," Ted says.

Shoot. I turn my face away from the sidewalk as

we turn in, but I know it's too late. Denham's seen me.

"What's he doing?" I ask Ted.

"Is that the guy?"

"Yes."

"He's staring at the car."

"Does he seem like he saw me?"

"He's following us on foot."

My heart races. "Don't park in the back. He'll know that's what we've been doing."

Ted abruptly turns into a spot at the side of the building. "He's pretty close. You want me to take him down?"

"No," I say. "Let me think."

I might as well look. Denham hangs out on the sidewalk a little longer, as if he's trying to decide what to do. We've turned so that my side of the car faces the street, so he's only a few yards away. Our eyes meet.

"He seems jumpy," Ted says.

"He does," I agree.

"I think I should have a word with him."

I hold out my arm. "No. Maybe I'll just skip dance."

"He might follow us."

"He doesn't have much gas," I say. But of course, that was yesterday. He might have filled up last night.

We continue to sit there, and then it seems like Denham makes up his mind. He steps into the parking lot, his face hard and determined. I think he's going to approach our SUV, but he storms past it and goes up the steps of the academy.

"That can't be good," I say.

"You want me to go in with you?" Ted asks.

"We could leave now," I say. "He couldn't follow."

Ted puts his hands on the gearshift to move into reverse, but I say, "Wait."

He settles back. "We'll wait."

The wind rushes through the trees in front of our windshield. I shiver. What is Denham doing in there? Demanding to see a list of all the four-year-old girls?

He can't know she's here. He just can't.

My phone buzzes. I pull it from my dance bag.

It's a text from Danika.

*Who is this man shouting in the halls about your daughter?*

My vision goes black for a moment. Oh my God. What is Denham doing?

I fling open the door and start running for the building. I can hear Ted's footsteps behind me. "Wait up," he orders. "I'm here for exactly this situation."

I don't slow down. By the time I hit the steps, though, Ted has caught up. "Let's be careful here," he says. "Crazies can do crazy things."

I nod. He tugs the door open.

Danika is in the foyer by the hall that leads to the studios, a phone in her hand. She sees me and waves me over.

Into the phone she says, "I don't know what he wants, but I'm concerned about the safety of the children here."

She looks at me and points to the phone. "The police."

I peer around her. Denham is standing on one of the benches by the dance rooms. The hall is otherwise empty, and I can see parents have moved into the studios to avoid him.

"What I WANT to KNOW," Denham yells, his voice loud and hoarse. "Is WHERE the hidden CHILD has gone! She belongs to LIVIA MASON. She is FOUR YEARS OLD! And I know SOMEBODY here knows WHERE she IS!"

"I can probably take him down," Ted says.

Danika looks over at him, then at me. "Who is that?" she asks. Then into the phone, "Thank you, we'll watch for the squad car. I'll stay on the line."

"A bodyguard," I answer.

Danika's eyes travel the length of Ted's body, up and down. "Looks like it," she says, then turns back to the hall.

"Suze!" she calls to the woman at the front desk. "Get on the intercom and tell everyone to stay in the studios."

Suze nods, her blond hair bobbing. She looks terrified.

"I don't think he'll hurt anybody," I say to Danika.

"You know him?" Danika looks at me.

But before I can explain, Denham spots me.

"THERE is LIVIA MASON!" Denham shouts, pointing in my direction. "THE CHILD will look like HER!"

I start to head for him, but Danika's arm shoots out to stop me. "He's crazy," she says. "Don't go near him."

"I know him," I say. "He lived with my family for a while when I was a teen."

Danika's eyes search my face for a moment, then she says into the phone, "I have someone here who can identify him." She hands me the phone. "Tell them his name."

I shakily take the phone, watching Denham. He's quit shouting, watching me. "He's not dangerous," I say, although I probably shouldn't. I don't know that. "His name is Denham Young. He's twenty-one. I don't think he lives here in San Antonio. He lived with my family five years ago in Houston."

Denham hops off the bench and heads my way. The bodyguard steps in front of me. "Don't even think about approaching her," he says, his voice low and menacing.

On the phone, a woman asks, "How long did you know him?"

"Your boyfriend hire this goon?" Denham asks.

I can't manage all these conversations at once. "A few months," I say into the phone, then pass it back to Danika. I don't answer Denham.

Denham tries to look at me around the rather formidable width of Ted. "Tell me where she is, Livia. I have a right to know where my baby is."

"You can't do this here," I say shakily. "This is just where I dance. Nobody here even knows about her."

"You know what he's talking about?" Danika asks.

I want to melt into a puddle on the floor. Everyone is looking at me. Danika. Suze. Ted. Denham. Thankfully the parents can't hear with the soundproofing.

"Denham, let's just go," I say. "The police are on their way and your record is already pretty bad."

"I don't care how much I inconvenience you," Denham says. "This isn't about you and me anymore. It's about our child."

"Our child is gone," I say.

Danika's head whips around. "You had a baby with this man? You're barely nineteen!"

Even Ted's expression flickers slightly as he continues to act as a shield between me and Denham.

"I can't believe you're doing this to me," I tell him. "I've kept this secret for four years, and you're destroying my life."

"Your life is a lie," Denham says. "And I aim to find my daughter."

"Not on my property, you won't," Danika says. "The police are on their way, and I'll be filing a restraining order against you immediately. Step foot in our parking lot, and I'll have you arrested every single time."

Denham finally tears his gaze from me to look at her. "I have no beef with you, lady," he says. "But I'm going to find out where my baby girl is." He pushes past Ted, who turns to keep himself between me and Denham. "And there isn't a damn thing you can do about it."

He stalks out of the door and down the steps.

"He's leaving," Danika says into the phone. "But I want to make sure he's not just going to his truck to get a weapon or anything crazy."

I know Denham won't do anything like that. He's just determined. And even though he is going about it the wrong way, I get what he wants. It's what drove me to look for Gabriella myself, to set up that fake profile, to watch her grow up.

Once you have a child out there in the world, it's hard to not think about them all the time. And Denham is going crazy with what he didn't even know he'd lost.

# Chapter Sixteen

Danika stands by the windows and watches Denham start up his truck and drive down the street. "He's gone," she says into the phone. "But that doesn't mean he won't be back."

She looks over her shoulder at me, her spiky blue hair lit by the sun streaming in. The creases around her eyes and mouth are more prominent while she's under stress. She's like the mother hen to all of us, the owner of the academy and the one who is willing to help any of us when we're in trouble.

"All right. Thank you." Danika hangs up the call. She turns around to me, Suze, and Ted, who are standing nearby, plus a couple parents who have ventured out of the studios.

"Should we send everyone home?" Suze asks.

Danika turns back to the windows. "Probably

most of them will go on their own," she says. "We'll need to send an email out to every family who attended this session, assuring them we are handling the situation." She glances at me. "Livia, when the officer gets here, we'll need to talk to him."

"I'll let everyone know it's safe to leave," Suze says, hurrying back to the front desk.

Ted moves close to me. "I can stand watch here," Ted says.

"That's good," Danika says.

Parents and children start streaming out of the hallway. Danika greets them, hugging the children, assuring everyone things are fine now, it was just some confused man.

A few older children remain in the rooms, their parents having run out to do errands during their class. Danika heads back to talk to the instructors, leaving me and Ted by the windows.

"I didn't see that coming, but I should have," I say to him.

"I see why Blitz wanted you protected," he says.

"He wouldn't hurt me," I insist.

"He seems pretty desperate," Ted says. "If he's willing to make a scene like that and risk getting arrested, there's a good chance he'd try to kidnap you or something."

"But I was in his truck yesterday," I say. "He could have taken off then, and he didn't."

"He's been stewing in it," Ted says. "He'll just get himself more and more worked up."

I don't have anything to say to that and watch out front until Danika returns.

"Where is that officer?" she asks. "Good thing we didn't actually need his help!"

"You were downgraded when the situation resolved," Ted says. "Non-emergency stop."

"Oh," Danika says. "Why don't you have Suze direct the officer to my desk when he gets here? Suze will know where to send him." She gestures back at the front desk.

"Will do," Ted says. He stands stalwart by the door, his hands clasped behind his back. "If you have any other entrances, you might want to secure them."

Danika turns to Suze. "Go lock the backstage doors and make sure the loading dock bay is secure."

Suze nods and grabs a set of keys from her drawer.

I follow Danika back through the doors to the recital hall, then turn toward her office. It's the opposite side of the building from the studios, so everything is quiet.

Danika settles in her chair, then props her elbows on the desk and rests her head in her hands. "That was something."

She seems weary, coming down from the adrenaline rush of the conflict.

"I'm so sorry that happened," I say. "He's been sitting out there for days. I should have told you."

"Days?" Her head pops up. "What is going on, Livia?"

I look down at my lap, fiddling with the sheer fabric of my dance skirt. "His name is Denham Young. He lived with me when I was a teenager. At the time, our family was told that he was my father's illegitimate son."

"Okay," Danika says. "So why is he here now?"

"He saw me on television and followed the trail to the academy after the video Blitz made. He's been stalking me a bit."

"You had a baby with him?"

My hands clasp together in a bruising grip. I don't have a choice anymore. I have to tell Danika. "He came to tell me that he wasn't my brother after all. We, well, we sort of had a ... relationship back then. I got pregnant and gave the baby up for adoption."

Danika sat back. "This is why your father acts the way he does, I take it?"

I nod. "Denham didn't know about the baby until he came back. My father sent him away before we found out I was pregnant."

"So he never signed anything giving up the baby?" Danika's face goes pale.

"No. Blitz is having his lawyer help us with it."

Danika rubs her forehead as if she's nursing a headache. "Do you know where the child is, Livia? Is that why he's doing this to you?"

"He's just guessing. He doesn't know what I know." I can't bring myself to tell her the rest. If she finds out about Gabriella, I just know she'll stop our lessons.

"But do you know where she is?" Danika's eyes are piercing.

"Yes," I say. "I've followed them on Facebook." It's not in me to lie, but I pray she doesn't ask if she is here at the academy.

"Then you need some protection or he'll get it out of you," she says. "I'm going to get a restraining order against him for the academy, not that I think it will do that much good. We'll probably hire some security for a little while, until this blows over." She turns to her computer.

"I'm so sorry this has happened," I say. "I had no idea he would find me."

She waves her hand. "We'll deal with it."

"Do you want me to stop coming?" I ask, fear in my voice.

"I don't know that it will matter. He might show

up anyway if he has nowhere else to look." She starts tapping on her keyboard.

"Okay."

"Stay here until the officer arrives, and we'll tell him all this," she says. "I'll let Bennett handle finding a security team for us. We'll get them in place by tomorrow."

"Ted can stay here through the last classes," I say. "He's hired full-time anyway."

"When does Blitz get back?"

"Tonight."

Danika nods. "All right. You and Ted stay here until we close, then you can take him with you. We'll get someone in place after that."

She goes quiet, staring at her screen. I sit quietly on my chair, reliving the past half hour, wondering how in the world my life has come to this.

## Chapter Seventeen

Blitz is on his way to the hotel by the time Ted and I leave Dreamcatcher. I know he's angry by his texts, which are abrupt and coming at a frenzied pace.

*I AM SO GOING TO TAKE THIS GUY OUT.*

*I should have creamed him when I had him on the ground.*

*This is outrageous. He could have done anything.*

*I'm going to pummel him into next week.*

THE SKY HAS GONE DARK BY THE TIME WE PULL UP to the valet in front of the hotel. Ted gets out. "I'm taking you up," he says when I turn to protest. "If anyone has Tweeted that they've seen Blitz here, that guy will turn up."

I have to give in. Blitz is still on his way. I shouldn't go anywhere alone, even the inside of the hotel.

We head up the elevator to the floor of suites. Ted stands in his menacing position, hands behind his back, cracking his knuckles as if he's going to have to fight somebody as soon as the doors open.

But the upstairs foyer is empty other than the bartender behind the private bar. "Anyone need a drink?" he asks when he sees us.

Both Ted and I give a grunting half-laugh to that, and then laugh for real at the other's reaction.

"We can wait out here," I tell Ted. "It's a secure floor." I don't really want to go into the suite with Ted. It feels too private.

"You got any coffee back there?" Ted asks.

"I can brew you some right up," the man says, turning to the back wall. "Anything for the lady?"

"No, thank you," I say, flopping onto the leather sofa opposite a television. It's showing a rerun of *I Love Lucy*. I remember it from my childhood, before I was banned from television by my father. Perfect, I think. Mindless comedy.

Ted sits on a stool by the bar, facing the elevators.

I wonder how he got into bodyguard work. But I'm not up for conversation.

I watch Lucy stomping grapes and try to relax.

The bartender has just poured a cup of coffee for Ted when the elevator opens and Blitz rushes out. He barrels toward the suite, then spots me on the sofa and stops dead. "Livia?"

I stand up, and then I'm in his arms, lifted off the ground.

"Are you okay? He didn't hurt you in any way, did he?" Blitz sets me down and looks me over, my arms, my face.

"He didn't lay a hand on her," Ted says. "I would have broken him in two."

"Theodore Banks!" Blitz says. "I was hoping they would send you!" They smack each other on the back. "How's life as a heavy?"

Ted shrugs. "Keeps me working." He sits back on his stool.

Blitz pulls me close, his arm around my waist, as he asks, "So what the hell happened?"

Ted sniffs. "The buffoon is walking out on the sidewalk when he spots your girl here in the SUV. I think he's going to approach us, but then he goes in the building instead. He makes a big scene, yelling and screaming in the halls, until the chick that owns the place calls the cops. She had me stand guard until they closed. Livia stayed with me."

"Shit," Blitz says. "Did he get arrested?"

"Nah, he took off."

Blitz holds me tighter. "Livia, what did Danika say?"

"She's getting a restraining order on him and hiring security until it blows over."

Blitz kisses my temple. "I'm sorry, baby."

Ted sips his coffee, then says, "You going to get a protective order for her too?"

Blitz shakes his head. "I think it's pointless and will make her name part of the public record, which could make things worse." He frowns. "I want to keep her under wraps as long as possible."

"You think he's got some loser pals he might bring along next time?" Ted asks.

Blitz looks at me. "What do you think, Livia? Would Denham call in reinforcements?"

I shrug. "I don't know anything about his life now," I say. "But he was always very good at making fast friends. Loyal friends."

"Ride-or-die types," Ted says. "Assholes with nothing to lose who get a charge out of stirring up trouble."

"He's only been out of jail a few months," Blitz says. "Do you remember the timeline from the list the lawyer sent? He could be on probation and violating it would send him back."

I shake my head. "I didn't pay that close attention. But he shouldn't know anybody here in San Antonio. I'm pretty sure he drove up here from Houston."

"And we have no idea where he went," Ted says.

"No," I say. "And I don't have any way to contact him either."

"Don't do that," both Ted and Blitz say simultaneously, then laugh.

"Same as old times," Blitz says.

"How do you two know each other?" I ask.

"Wrestling," Blitz says. "We were both on the high school team."

I look back and forth between them. Blitz is muscled and strong, but has a lean dancer's body. Ted is like a brick wall. "How did that work out?"

Ted answers. "We didn't compete against each other. He was a totally different weight class."

"I could have taken you," Blitz says.

Now Ted's laugh is a roar. He's lost all the gruffness he's had with me all day. "I could squash you like a bug."

Blitz holds up his hands. "I could wriggle out of those sloppy meat-hook hands of yours any day."

I lean my head on Blitz's shoulder. It's nice to

have an easy moment after these horrible two days. He squeezes my waist again. "I think we're going to head out," he says to Ted. "I should be able to take it from here. Thanks for watching out for her."

Ted stands up from the stool. "No prob." He shakes Blitz's hand. "Let me know if you need me again."

"Will do." Blitz's face flashes dark for a moment. "Will definitely do."

Ted heads to the elevator, and Blitz and I walk toward our suite.

"Something's wrong," I say. "Why do you think you'll need Ted again? Do you have to go back to LA?"

Blitz opens our door. "We're going to be doing some publicity stuff for the DVD release," he says. "I just think a few extra eyes will be good."

"You said 'we' just now," I say. "You mean both of us?" My belly quakes. I can't imagine being out in public with reporters or even strangers with cell phones, recording an outburst with Denham. I was lucky today. It was still relatively secret.

"I'm trying to work things out still," Blitz says. "The lawyers can sort it." He perches against the back of the sofa and draws me to him. "Meanwhile, I haven't seen you in two whole days."

His lips press into the sensitive skin below my ear,

and my anxiety begins to drift away. By the time he has his mouth fully on mine, I've let go of the afternoon. I've missed him, desperately, and now I can sink back into his attention.

"I love you in pale blue," Blitz whispers into my ear, tugging the neckline of the stretchy leotard until it bares my shoulder. "Although I think I like you out of it even better."

My body warms to his hot kisses along my collarbone. He pulls both shoulders of the leotard down and pulls my arms out, first one, then the other.

"I'm going to kiss every part of you," he says, baring my body, inch by inch. The leotard slides to my waist. He takes both breasts in his hands and his mouth trails down to take a nipple in his mouth. "I missed these," he says.

I wrap my arms around his neck, eyes closed, reveling in the feel of Blitz. His hair tickles my skin, and I catch the smell of him that is so familiar, pine and leather.

He removes the black vest as he works, kicking off his shoes. Then he kneels in front of me, reaching down for the Crocs I wear to the studio before I change into ballet slippers. He eases them off.

His hands grasp the leotard, which is at my waist now, and jerk everything down, tights and all. For a moment I'm bound at the knees, but Blitz lifts my leg to tug one side the rest of the way down.

Before he reaches for the other, though, he takes advantage of my parted thighs to bury his face there. His tongue slides along me, and I have to clutch the back of the sofa to keep my balance.

"Mmm," he says. "There's no place like home."

He pulls the tights off my other leg and stands up. "Now I've got you where I want you."

He lifts me up into his arms. "To the bedroom with us."

His footsteps are silent as we move from the living room to the bed. He nudges aside the sheer drapes that surround it, and slides me onto the mattress. I watch him as he slides off his pants, shirt, and boxers.

Then he crawls between the silks over to me. "Think the bartender out there is tired of hearing you cry out?" he asks.

"I think the walls are pretty thick," I say.

"Mmm," he says. "Let's test them."

And as his mouth works back down my body, he does exactly that.

# Chapter Eighteen

It's a relief to have Blitz back. The weekend means no dance classes, but Blitz decides we should dance somewhere other than Dreamcatcher on the days we don't have Gabriella to see.

His manager's assistant sends profile after profile of ballet instructors in San Antonio, plus others willing to travel. We sit cross-legged on the bed with his computer, reading over the qualifications of the teachers, but my heart isn't really in it.

"This one could teach us ballet lifts," Blitz says, turning the screen to me.

"We've been wanting to do that," I say absently.

Blitz shuts the lid of the laptop. "Come here, baby," he says. "This has been the worst week, hasn't it?"

He pulls me into his arms, and we lie side by side

on the enormous bed. Morning is long past, but we haven't gone anywhere, just soaking in each other's presence, lounging in soft thick robes and eating room service.

His fingers tangle through my hair. "I guess it's not the worst week of your life, though," he says. "Is it?"

I shake my head against his shoulder.

"You want to tell me about the worst?" he asks.

I'm not sure I do, but he waits so patiently that I find it is easy to release the memories to him.

"Denham and I didn't have a lot of time together before it blew up," I say. "That week was the worst week."

The bad days flood back. August, really, was our month, the week before school started, when he taught me to drive, then the first weeks of school when we were messing around, and finally became lovers.

Late September was when it all fell apart.

Denham and I were like magnets, unable to pull away from each other. We joined clubs at school, and stayed for homework help, anything to spend less time at home. We would duck out early, buying ourselves time before we were expected home.

Denham had friends all over, and we borrowed their bedrooms, their cars, and finally discovered a broken-down travel trailer in the backyard of a neighbor, unlocked and unused.

It became our space.

The dark period of my life began when Denham confessed to me that we shared a father. We were in the trailer, cuddled up on the narrow bed with a blanket we'd brought and kept there.

I was talking about Andy, who had just turned four. He had asked for a black leather jacket so he could "be like his brother."

"You're so good with him," I told Denham. "It's like you really are his brother."

His face contorted at that and a strangled sound came out of his throat.

"Denham? What's wrong?" We were naked, as usual, and when I sat up, the blanket fell to my waist.

He glanced at my body, then covered me as if he couldn't bear to look at me. "Livia, we can't do this anymore."

This made me sit up. "What do you mean? I love you. You love me! That is all that matters."

"No," he said, shifting away. "That's not all that matters. Shit."

He shoved the blanket away and set his feet on the floor. He sat hunched over, his head in his hands.

I curled around him, my cheek on his back. "What else matters?"

"Family," he said. "Your parents have been good to me. And Andy. God, that little kid. Everything he knows is a lie."

My heartbeat slammed in my ears. I had no idea what he could be talking about, but his voice was scaring me.

He stood up, forcing me to break away from him. A streetlamp on the corner formed pale lines across his skin from the blinds. I couldn't make out his face.

"I treat Andy like a brother because he IS my brother, Livia. The reason I live with your family now is because your dad is my dad."

I held the blanket to my chest, not sure I understood. The words were too much, spilling over like a pitcher that was too full. "What are you saying, Denham?"

He stepped close to me then and took my shoulders in his hands, gripping them like a vise. "I'm your brother, Livia. Your half-brother. Your father was with my mother. She had me. That's why I'm here now."

My body revolted. I started dry-heaving, clutching my belly, my breath coming in pants.

"Livia, I'm sorry. I should have stayed away. I should have." Denham tried to hold me, but I curled in on myself. I was blindsided by pain. Everything hurt. My belly. My burning eyes. My heart felt ready to burst.

"Talk to me, Livia. Say you don't hate me."

But I couldn't speak. I couldn't talk at all. I huddled, trying to manage the trauma and the pain. It was horrible. He was my brother. And we did things. All the things. Everything.

I could still feel my body, swollen and slightly sore from this last time, just a few minutes ago.

He knew all along, and yet he did those things, over and over.

To his sister.

I flung him away. I didn't even stop for my clothes, but wrapped myself tightly in the blanket and flew out of the trailer.

The ground was cold and wet on my bare feet.

I ducked through the broken slats of the fence and crossed the small alley to get to our own backyard. I opened the gate to the fence and raced across the yard to the back door.

I wanted nothing more than to go to my room and be alone, but everyone was right inside. Mom, Dad, and Andy sat at the dinner table. Denham and I were supposed to be at a football game.

Dad saw me in the blanket, eyes on my bare legs and feet. The blanket slipped, exposing my bare shoulder.

"Oh my God," he said. "Who did this to you?" He turned to Mom. "Call the police."

"No!" I cried. "Just leave me alone!" I tried to run past, but Dad caught me.

"Baby," he said. "Let us help you. What happened?"

Andy started to cry, and Mom picked him up.

I didn't want to talk, but I did want the truth.

"Is Denham really your son?"

His face bloomed red. Mom clutched Andy, her eyes wide.

"Tell me!" I said to Dad. "Is he?"

"Where is that boy?" Dad roared.

"I won't tell you until you answer me!" I shouted back. I had to know, but I could already see it. I could tell by Dad's anger, his upset, Mom's shock.

"Ray?" Mom managed to say. "Is that why he's here?"

Dad turned to her, his mouth opening and closing as if he was trying to find the right words.

"Oh my God," I said. "Oh my God, oh my God, oh my God." I broke away from Dad then, and that time he let me go.

"What has he done?" Mom said. "What has that evil child done to our little girl?"

She followed after me, but I was well ahead and closed the door and locked it. I threw the blanket aside and grabbed clothes as fast as I could. I should have gotten dressed. I'd made it obvious what happened. I didn't think.

Mom knocked on my door, but I ignored her, dragging on jeans and a sweatshirt, then burying myself beneath the covers.

The doorknob jiggled, then stopped. I thought she'd given up. But then I heard a sharp bang against the metal. I realized she was in. She'd jimmied the lock.

"Come here," Mom said, wrapping her arms around me. I stayed in my ball beneath the covers. "You'll be all right. We'll take care of it."

A door slammed out in the house, then a car started.

They wouldn't find him. Nobody knew about the trailer. Surely Denham would hide out there.

Unless he thought I would tell them where he was.

I rocked back and forth beneath the covers. Denham had friends. He'd find someplace to go.

But then I realized I'd lost him. Denham. My love. My sweet, sweet love.

My emotions crashed against each other. Betrayal, anger, devastation, loss. I loved him. But we were related. It couldn't be. I couldn't go after him. He was gone. I sobbed and sobbed into my pillow, my body curled around it, my mom's hands on my back.

Then I heard Andy crying, softly saying, "Livia, Livia, Livia," over and over again.

This got to me and I shoved the blanket aside enough that he could crawl in with me. His little arms went around my neck and clutched me like he was drowning. I rocked with him, our mother wrapping herself around us, until he fell asleep.

Eventually Mom took him to his bed. The house was eerily quiet. My hair spun wild and snarled around my face. My skin was hot and damp from crying and sweating beneath the blankets. I slid to the floor, my back against the bed.

My body was still tender from the last time Denham and I were together. The last time. It was over. A cry bubbled up from my chest, but there weren't any tears left. I was too dehydrated, too tired.

Mom came back into the room and sat on the floor next to me. She took my hand and we just existed for a while as she hummed softly.

Finally, she asked, "Did he force you?"

I shook my head no.

"Did he hurt you in any way?"

I shook my head again, although my heart was certainly in unimaginable pain.

She sighed. "Okay, so how far did it go?"

I didn't want to answer that. That it went every way, every distance, over and over again, night after night, stolen moment after stolen moment. That I loved him completely, and had given myself over to him totally.

"I'm going to assume pretty far," she said. "We'll need to get you to a doctor. God, you're so young. Did you even know what was happening?"

I let go of her and covered my eyes with my hand. I couldn't handle those questions. It was too much for one night. Way too much.

"All right," she said. "Let's get you in bed. There will be time enough to face all this tomorrow."

She stood up and took my arm to lift me up as well. I lay on the bed fully dressed, but she still covered me with the blanket.

Mom was at the doorway when I finally found the voice to ask, "What will happen to Denham?"

She shook her head. "I don't know, Livia. But he won't be coming back here."

I buried my face in the pillow as she closed the door. I was wrong. There were more tears. So many more. A whole ocean of them, just out to tide, and now they spilled all over again.

~*~*~

Blitz lazily strokes my hair as I finish this part of the story.

"I'm so sorry, Princess," he says. "That is more than anyone could live through."

I turn my face into his robe, letting the soft white cotton absorb any stray tears so that he won't see them. I don't want to cry about Denham in the presence of Blitz. My life is good now, perfect, full of love and dance and time with my daughter.

But the young version of me, the not-quite-fifteen-year-old with her first broken heart, traumatized and lied to, still hurts after all these years.

"Did your dad throw him out?" Blitz asks. "What happened?"

"Dad came back early in the morning," I say. "He got Denham's things together in garbage bags and shoved them in his car. He told us he took Denham back to his Aunt Didi. I'm guessing that he did, but his aunt must have called CPS because he ended up in foster care. At least that's what he said."

"I remember him saying that," Blitz says. "That's how he got the DNA test." He exhales slowly. "Hell of a thing. And you had to live all those years thinking he was your brother."

"None of us had any way to know otherwise. I guess Dad could have done the DNA test himself. I think it was available then."

"Not easily," Blitz says.

I nod against his shoulder. If only he had. My life would have played out so differently.

"When did you find out about the baby?" Blitz asks.

"A few weeks later. I was a pretty big wreck. Not eating. Missing school. Feeling sick. I lost a lot of weight. So nothing was obvious for a while."

"How did you know then?"

"I was throwing up a lot. Mom got worried. She took me to the doctor. Dad was flipping out, and demanded to know when it happened. I think he thought we were still finding a way to see each other."

"Did Denham ever try to contact you?" Blitz asks.

"No. I didn't hear from him again until that day he showed up here."

"You didn't look for him either?"

"He was my brother. There was no point. And I had no way to do it. Dad pulled me out of school, got a new job here in San Antonio, and then it was house arrest until I met you. No television, no social media, no computer, very little contact with the outside world. He thought he could purify me, make me innocent again. I don't know."

"He chose that teeny tiny church on purpose."

"Yes. It was an elderly church, no young families, sort of dying out. Perfect for a father who wanted to keep his teenaged daughter away from anyone her own age."

"Jesus, Livia. It must have been so lonely."

I shift onto my back, watching the silks on the bed flutter lightly. "I got used to it. And eventually Mom wanted us to have some social interaction, so I met my friend Mindy. She was homeschooled too and had a younger brother who could be Andy's friend."

"You haven't seen her since I came along." Blitz reaches for a long lock of my hair and twirls it around his fingers.

"She got grounded, her phone taken away. I don't have any way to reach her unless I just storm up to her door."

"Maybe I'll pose as a pizza delivery man," Blitz says. "Steal her away."

"I do want to see her. But she is only sixteen, and her parents still control her."

Blitz draws me back to him. "We're going to make everything right, Livia. All of it."

I turn in to his body, strong and stalwart beside me. I love that he says this to me, even though I don't see how it could happen. Denham could do anything in his desperation. In this world where anybody can go viral, we're just one Tweet away from the whole world knowing what happened to Blitz Craven's new girl when she was fifteen.

# Chapter Nineteen

On Monday Blitz drives us across town to Jenica's Dancery, a hip contemporary ballet studio.

Blitz is extremely pumped to have found this woman, who was classically trained and performed with the LA Ballet before creating a fusion style all her own.

"She'll be perfect," he says. "We can learn lifts and grow in a brand-new style."

I hug my purple Dreamcatcher Dance Academy bag to my chest and try not to feel nervous. I am barely into *pointe* shoes, and here we are going to a new dance space to be assessed by an instructor I've never met.

We pull up to a boxy, flat-roofed building. Every

car in the lot looks like it has seen better days, and a half-dozen bicycles are chained to a rack by the door.

Blitz's excitement grows as we walk up to the door. "This is perfect," he says. "Authentic dancers, none of that Hollywood ego." He takes my hand and pulls on the handle.

"Don't you have your own trainers?" I ask. I remember the stilted woman on the set of *Dance Blitz* who was opposed to me going on the show.

"You're thinking of Amara, the choreographer of the show," Blitz says. "I only see her when we have an upcoming season, and right now we don't. My trainer quit after the shit storm."

We enter a space that could only be described as rustic. The floor is bare, cracked concrete, and the walls rough-hewn cedar for about eight feet, then the soaring ceiling is corrugated metal. A makeshift desk sits right by the door, built from wood planks and cinder blocks.

Huge photos with curling corners are tacked to the back wall, which is only about ten feet from the entrance, making the room feel smashed. There are doors on either end.

A girl in a black leotard and tights with slashes through them comes out one of the doors. Her white-blond hair is slicked back into the tiniest sprig of a ponytail. She sees Blitz and obviously recognizes him immediately, because she says, "Are you serious?"

Blitz holds out his hands and smiles. "As a heart attack!" He drapes his arm around my waist. "I'm guessing you aren't Jenica."

"Omigawd, Jen let you in here?" Her hands tighten into fists. "She said she would never sell out!"

My ire starts to hit a fever pitch and I want to slug her. But before I can say or do anything, Blitz simply says, "I'm guessing you aren't going to help us find her, so maybe we'll just show ourselves around."

A shirtless man in dance tights and jazz shoes steps out from the door behind her and spots Blitz. "Holy hell, it's Blitz Craven!" He hurries forward to clasp Blitz's hand and shakes it vigorously. "It's an honor, man, a serious honor." He realizes he's shaken too long and lets go, running his palms across the shiny satin surface of his skullcap. "You looking for Jen?"

"We are," Blitz says. "Is she around somewhere?"

"She's in the studio," he says. "She know you're coming?"

The girl in black lets out a huge sigh and plunks down on the exercise ball behind the desk. She jerks open a box on the floor and pulls out an iPad.

"I don't think she's as glad to see me," Blitz says conspiratorially.

"Weeza isn't glad to see much of anyone," the guy says. "I'm Corey."

"Nice to meet you, Corey," Blitz says. "Lead the way." He gestures for the door.

I flash one more angry look back at Weeza. What sort of name is that anyway? She doesn't look up from the iPad, the screen full of colored squares like the scheduling software Suze uses at Dreamcatcher. I feel a pang of grief that we're here and not there.

We pass through the door, which opens into a huge multi-use room the size of a gymnasium. There are high mats and ribbons hanging from the ceiling in one corner. A woman is pushing off the mat, her arms wound in the silks.

Along the back wall is a mirror and a barre that must be twenty feet long. There are two different groups using it, a half-dozen young women all dressed in flesh-colored leotards that make you look twice. And two male-female couples at the other end, stretching each other with the barre to steady them.

In the center are three small trampolines. A muscular man is doing flips between them, landing cleanly on one and bouncing to the other. And in the far corner, near the other door, a couple is dancing to the actual music that blares through the speakers, a stunning contemporary dance with very high tosses and dramatic falls.

A woman with blond-brown hair twisted into an elegant chignon directs the dancing couple. She is striking in a deep scarlet leotard and long skirt made of separate jewel-toned scarves.

Corey has paused to let us take in the space, but now he leads us over to the woman in scarlet. I assume this is Jenica.

Corey taps her shoulder. She turns and I realize she is younger than I figured, only in her thirties. "Blitz!" she says, extending her arms. "I'm so glad you made it over."

She embraces him, then turns back to the couple. "Ferris and Gina, work on the lift in the second chorus. I'll be back in a moment."

The couple nods at her. The music abruptly stops and starts again mid-song. I haven't spotted where it's coming from yet, but obviously someone controls it.

"This must be Livia," Jenica says, reaching out to grasp both my hands. Her skin is chilly despite the warm room. "So lovely. I saw you on the show. Have you been *en pointe* long? It looked new."

"Just a few weeks," I say. "I probably shouldn't have done it then."

"You were perfect," she says. "We can get you stronger on them. Did you bring a pair?"

I pat my bag. "Of course."

She turns back to Blitz. "And you want to learn

lifts. I think I'll pair you with Gina there." She gestures back at the couple right as the man, Ferris, tosses the girl perilously high. "She has a lot of experience and can get you ready to work with Livia." She pats his arm. "You're strong, but we'll need you stronger!"

"Weeza didn't exactly give them a warm welcome," Corey says. "Just so you know."

"Oh, Weeza doesn't welcome anyone," Jenica says with a wave of her hand. "I'm sure Blitz is familiar with professional disdain." Her smile makes her eyes sparkle. "Let's dive right in. Livia, go warm up at the barre with the girls over there. I'll introduce you. Blitz, Corey will warm you up until Gina is ready for you."

And just like that, Blitz and I are separated, and I have a new class and instructor. I glance back at him, unsure and anxious. Dreamcatcher was the last little bit of my old life. I feel as untethered as I have ever been.

Jenica walks me over to the women in the skin-colored leotards. "This is Livia," she says. "She just began *en pointe* and needs more strength and flexibility. Take good care of her."

The girls glance over at me and continue their *pliés*, except for the last one, who breaks away. "I'm Ingrid. I lead this group. You can change into shoes."

I realize none of the other girls are in *pointe* shoes at the moment, so I put on a pair of regular ballet slippers.

"We have a set routine for warm-up," Ingrid says. "We're all old hat at it now, but I'll talk you through it. You'll have it memorized eventually."

She gives me commands, all traditional ballet movements that I thankfully know. I have to concentrate on staying with the other girls, so I can't try to spot Blitz in the mirror to see how he is doing with this other girl.

Jealousy and a spot of fear burns in my belly. It was one thing when I had Blitz to myself. Dreamcatcher was mostly a children's academy, with only a few older teen and adult classes.

But this studio is completely different. They are all beautiful young people with a passion for dance. I feel out of place, an old-fashioned wallflower in a room full of dazzle.

I force myself to pay attention. There is no place for jealousy here, only determination and drive. The other girls are sharply focused, their movements perfectly in sync, each position a flawless example of a pose.

"We have to master the basics before we can break the rules," Ingrid says, not to me, but to all of us. "When we achieve perfection in the classics, we can give wings to our fresh approach."

Between her encouragements, Ingrid prompts me on the next move. I am not quite in time with the others, having to move into position once I hear the command. But I begin to feel their silent count, the rhythm to their pace that is independent of the music playing overhead.

"All of it, again," Ingrid says. "Keep your form no matter how you tire."

I begin to be able to predict the next motion, and eventually we overlap what we did before. I become more confident in the poses, and Ingrid gives me less prompting. "Good, Livia," she says. "You are getting it."

The work is far more challenging than the routine Betsy puts us through, and by the time the sequence begins again, many parts of me are screaming. I manage to glance into the mirror to find Blitz. He has the Gina girl in the air, with Corey and Ferris spotting her as Blitz makes a turn, his arms extended.

His hands are on the girl's rib cage and thigh, and jealousy burns into me again. I want to be the girl he lifts.

I lose my rhythm and fall a beat behind, then have to scramble to catch back up. Ingrid's eye flashes over to me for an instant, but she says nothing. She works alongside us, matching every move we do.

When we come to the end of the sequence a third time, she sends us to the floor. I want to groan with relief. Blitz is standing next to Ferris now, nodding as he's instructed on a hand position. Jenica watches from the side. She sees me looking at Blitz and winks.

I quickly look down at my knee as we move into a floor stretch.

I'm not really sure how long we work out. The lights never flicker, and no hour is ever counted down. New people arrive in other corners, others leave.

Finally, Blitz comes over. "I'm apparently no longer safe to lift a ham sandwich," he says to me, looking over the girls. "I totally need to buy you one of those naked leotards."

My cheeks burn and a couple of the other girls laugh a little. We continue our stretch, and Blitz sits down next to me to follow our lead.

Eventually Ingrid stands. "Tomorrow, we do *pointe*, so bring your shoes."

I guess we're done.

When I stand up, my legs are wobbly. Blitz notices and laughs. "You too, Princess?"

He helps pull me up as Jenica comes over.

"I think you had a good first day," she says. "We

expect you tomorrow. We'll work out the soreness you will feel."

Blitz rolls his shoulders. "Yeah, this is gonna burn," he says. He nudges me. "Race you to the masseuse."

Jenica shakes her head. "Young people with money," she says. "You are spoiled. We'll get you in proper dance shape."

Blitz waves at her as we collect my bag and head to the door. I'm too tired to even bend down and change my shoes, so I just shove my Crocs on over my slippers.

We pass by Weeza, who sits glaring at Blitz from behind her desk. He blows her a kiss. "Miss you," he says.

She slams her phone on the desktop. "Don't speak to me, Hollywood scum," she says.

"Please let me punch her, just once," I say.

Blitz leads me out the door. "Eh, she'll just make you go viral on Twitter. I'm saving that for when you give birth to Blitz, Jr."

I stop in my tracks. "What?"

He turns back to me and reaches for my hand. "Sorry, that was a really bad joke. I think all the lactic acid in my worn-out muscles has gone to my brain."

We head for the gray Mazda. My head is spinning. One, that Blitz wants a kid. Two, with me. And third, has he forgotten what we're going through right now?

I buckle in, not sure what to say. Blitz starts the car, then realizes I'm still quiet. He takes my hand and lifts my fingers to his lips. "I'm sorry, Livia. It was a boneheaded thing to say. I really wasn't thinking."

I nod at him and look out the side window. How easy it is for him to forget where I've been, the things I've had to do.

Gabriella's birth was the best and worst day of my life.

-*-*-

DAD WENT TO MY FIRST PRENATAL VISIT, WHERE WE confirmed the pregnancy. He hadn't spoken to me in the weeks since he sent Denham back to his aunt. He acted like I didn't exist.

Dad transformed completely. Angry. Quick to judgment. I was forbidden from going to school. My mom had to do the homeschool paperwork and get me unenrolled.

During a television show one night, two teenagers kissed and he grossly overreacted, yanking the plug from the wall and declaring no one in the family was going to watch that trash. He shoved the TV into the hall closet and took away my ancient desktop computer I once used for homework.

When the doctor suggested that I was still eligible for a first-trimester abortion, Dad stormed out. Within two days, he had resigned his job and ordered my mother to pack the house. We were moving.

The computer and television didn't move with us.

In San Antonio, Dad chose an elderly man to oversee my prenatal care, but he didn't come to appointments. Mom and I heard the heartbeat and saw the blips of the baby's shape on my sonograms.

Dad had ordered Mom to sit outside while I saw the doctor, but on this, she didn't listen to him and came in the exam room with me. They did, however, instruct everyone in the office not to tell me if I was having a boy or a girl. I didn't argue. At fifteen, I had no voice.

I was utterly alone for most of that year. Mom bought homeschool materials and expected me to be self-paced. I fell behind, but nobody pushed me right away. Andy was still young, of course, and stayed at home as well, but he kept calling me "fat" and nobody corrected him. I understood that he wasn't to be told the truth.

I'm sure other mothers feel wonder at the baby moving inside them, and there is a quiet joy in the kicks and the progression of their bellies from flat to beach ball.

But I had no one to be happy with. Only two upset parents and a little boy who didn't know. I sometimes thought of Denham and how differently I could have handled that night. But now we were in a new town, and I couldn't go anywhere. I was to be seen by no one.

I remember when my water broke. I'd felt contractions for weeks, random cramps that rippled across my belly. At first I was terrified, but when I told my parents, my father told me I deserved every pain I felt. Mom explained they were just for practice. I only hoped when the time came, I could tell the difference between those and the real ones.

I did. When the first labor contraction came three days after I was due, I called Mom in. It was mid-afternoon, and Dad was at work. She sat by me to time them, but it was almost half an hour before another one came. She said we'd wait until Dad came home to watch Andy, and then she'd take me up to the hospital.

With the third one, I felt warm and wet. I tried to stand up to avoid drenching my bed, but the pain was sharp and intense. I started huffing like I'd seen on sitcoms. I hadn't done a birthing class, as my father wouldn't let me out of the house other than for doctor visits. And even then, he'd always stood guard on the porch, making sure none of the neighbors saw me as I hurried from the house to the car. He ensured nobody in our new city knew, especially the neighbors.

Mom called him to come home early, but he said I could damn well live with the pain until he was good and ready to get there. He stayed an extra half hour, just to spite us.

I was crying with the pain by then. I barely weighed one hundred pounds even at nine months pregnant, young and small. I had trouble gaining weight. The whole ordeal was more than I could bear, and I was terribly scared.

Mom had finally loaded Andy in the car. He was whimpering with fear every time I cried out, when Dad drove up. They got in an awful fight over her disobeying him, but he took Andy and let us leave.

By the time we got to the hospital, I was too close to delivery to get an epidural. And still, the pushing went on and on. Mom wiped my forehead with washcloths. The nurses clucked over how young I was, so even between the rounds of pushing, I cried from embarrassment and shame.

When the baby's head started to come out, the nurse got the doctor and he sat at my knees to deliver the baby. I noticed another woman in the room, tall and sharp nosed, holding a folder flattened against her chest. She waited like a hawk.

The moment the baby was out, she stepped forward. I was trying to listen to the baby's first cry, to sit up and get a peek, when the woman's deadpan voice said, "Your parents have informed me you don't want to see the baby or know the gender."

My vision was a red haze of pain and exhaustion and relief. I ignored her. "Is it a boy or a girl?" I asked the doctor.

But the woman stepped forward again. "We really recommend you not see or hold the baby or know the gender prior to transfer to the adoptive parents. It makes the transition easier."

I looked over at Mom. She was biting her lip.

"Mom?" I asked her.

"You had to know we weren't going to keep it," she said.

I looked at the doctor, who had passed the baby on to a team who was wiping her down on a little table beneath a bright light.

"I want to know," I said. "Boy or girl?"

"Initial here that you acknowledged our consultation and chose not to follow our instructions." The woman stepped forward with the folder and a pen.

"Is this really the best way to go about it?" the doctor asked. "The poor girl has just had a baby!"

One of the nurses touched his arm. "It's how some of them do it," she said.

He shook his head. "Not on any of the deliveries I've done." He turned back to me. "Nurse, delivery of the placenta," he said.

I felt another push and a gush down below. I looked over at the table. The baby was crying, her face red. I could see she was a girl as they cleaned her. I sat back.

The doctor lowered my legs from the metal holders. "Time of birth, 8:52 p.m. Healthy baby *girl*." He glared up at the woman as he said it and stood up.

"Apgar is 6," one of the nurses with the baby said.

The doctor patted my leg. "You did all right."

"The couple is waiting downstairs," the tall woman said, still holding out her folder. "They wanted to be here for the birth. We just need the signatures so we can transfer parental rights."

I ignored her, looking over at the baby. They were wrapping her in a striped blanket. One of the nurses placed a small stretchy cap on her head.

"I want to hold her," I said. "I get to do that, right?"

The nurses looked at each other, frowning.

"I don't think it's a good idea," the woman said.

I pushed myself higher on the bed. "I want to hold her," I insisted.

One of the nurse aides, a short one with dark curly hair, brought her over to me. "Here you go," she said.

The moment I felt the featherlight weight of her, I was filled with wonder.

I couldn't see much of her, just her little face. She yawned sleepily, and it was the most amazing thing I'd ever seen. How did she know how to yawn?

Her cheeks were pinker than her forehead and her chin. She had short stubby lashes and almond-shaped eyes. I could have stared at her forever.

I looked up at Mom, to see if she felt the same awe, but she was sitting in the corner, focused on the parking lot outside the window instead.

I gazed back down. Her eyes were slate blue. I thought I could see his nose on her, but it was so small and round.

I couldn't hold her hands or see her feet in her burrito bundle, but it was enough to look at her face. A string on her little hat had unraveled, and I smoothed it down.

Such tiny ears. Little wisps of dark hair.

"We need to take her to be assessed," a nurse said. "Weighed and measured and a more thorough cleaning." She held out her arms.

I didn't want to let her go. I looked at her again. What if this was it? The only time I would see her? I desperately wished for a camera, a cell phone, anything that would capture this moment. But I had nothing, and no one in the room would do it for me. Not under these circumstances.

My throat tightened so hard that I could barely breathe. They couldn't take her. They just couldn't!

The woman with the folder cleared her throat. A stern-faced nurse, the one who told the doctor that this was all normal, forcibly took the baby from me. I wanted to hold on and tensed my arms, but she warned, "The baby is fragile."

So I let go.

*I let go.*

They placed her in a plastic crib on a rolling cart.

"She's losing her hat," one said, but they wheeled her out anyway.

She was gone.

"I have all the paperwork right here," the woman with the folder said.

"Mom?" I asked again. "Is this what you decided?"

"We can't keep the baby," she said. "It's an abomination."

Tears flowed down my face. She was not. She was perfect.

The woman held out the folder but I turned my face away.

"Just bring it here," Mom said.

"She's a minor," the woman said. "Here is where your signatures go. But we still want her to sign."

"I won't," I said.

A rumbling voice came from the doorway. It was my father, holding my brother Andy. "You will."

My insides quaked. He looked large and formidable in the stark room.

My joy at seeing the baby, and my resolve to fight them, crumbled. Andy squirmed in his arms, trying to get down to me, but my father held him tight.

"I'm just here to sign those papers, and then we'll leave," my father said.

He passed Andy to Mom and took the pages from her. He scribbled his name and brought the paper to me.

"Sign right here, Livia," he said.

My hands trembled on the sheets. I was coming down off the high of seeing the baby, and exhaustion was setting in. I wanted to be alone to cry.

I took the papers and found the line with "Birth mother" below it. I scrawled my name.

The woman flipped the page. "Also here and here, and initial these three places."

I did what I was told. There was nothing I could do anyway. Where does a fifteen-year-old go with a baby if she's kicked out of her house?

"Leave the baby's name blank," the woman said. "I'll get that from the adoptive family."

"I don't get to name her?" I asked.

"You should detach yourself as quickly as possible," the woman said. "It's for the best."

I lay back, starting to feel all the places in my body that throbbed. My boobs felt funny too, hot and tingly. If they were all going to stare at me like I was a monster, I would just as soon all of them leave.

"Are we square on the paperwork?" my dad asked.

The woman flipped through the pages again. "Yes, I already had most of it filled in." She picked up her bag from the corner. "I'll be in touch if I need anything else."

She whisked herself from the room.

"Come on, Dorothy," my dad said. "We can pick her up when they discharge her." He turned to the curly-haired aide, who had returned to quietly pick up the bedding and trays. "When will she get out?"

"Probably tomorrow," she said. "She's a minor. Are you sure you should leave her?"

"She's old enough to get in this situation," he said. "She's old enough to get through it on her own."

The aide bit her lip and flashed me a sympathetic glance. "We'll keep an eye on her."

My mom hadn't moved from the chair, her face

grave. "Ray, are you sure? She's our daughter, alone in a hospital."

"You will obey me," my father said. "Not a lick of you in this family knows how to handle themselves."

"A social worker will be coming," the aide said. "Standard procedure when a girl this young has a child."

My father turned to her. "I do NOT consent to anyone talking to her. Do you hear me? Nobody."

The aide bit her lip again, but didn't say a word.

"Come on, Dorothy," Dad said. He took Andy from her. "It's late and we need to get our son to bed."

Mom picked up her sweater and purse. "Your overnight bag is here," she said, patting the red duffel. "I'll call later and see how you are."

Dad grunted at that, striding for the door without a backward glance. Mom gave me a quick hug and followed him out.

When they were gone, the aide turned to me and helped me change into a new gown. "The social worker is required by law to come. If you've been abused or harmed, that would be the time to speak up."

When I was dressed again, I sank down in the bed. They were worried the baby was my father's, I guessed. I would assure them that wasn't true, and that everything that happened was my own decision.

But I would never ever tell them the truth. That part of the secret was something I agreed with my dad about. No one needed to know about Denham.

# Chapter Twenty

Blitz and I wake up Tuesday morning with groans and whimpers.

"I can't move my arms," Blitz says with a laugh. "Jenica killed me."

"My butt will never be the same," I tell him. "We did too many *arabesques* for a week, much less a day."

Blitz turns to me and rolls me onto my belly. "Well, rubbing your butt with my sore hands should help both of us, right?"

I laugh. "Maybe. Wait. Oww!" The pressure is like a bruise being punched. I reach and grab his upper arm and squeeze. "How is that?"

"Hurts so good," he says, collapsing back down on the bed. "We need a hot tub in our room."

I lean up on one elbow. Even that sends a howl

through my midsection. "Why don't we have a hot tub in our room? Did you get cheap on me?"

His chest rumbles with a throaty chuckle. "I think there are jets in the bathtub, actually."

I drop back on the pillow. "Then call somebody to come fill it," I say.

Blitz drops a kiss on my forehead. "Being spoiled agrees with you," he says. "How about I go get a steaming, jet-powered bath going for us?"

I drag myself to sitting. "I'll help," I say, grimacing at all the places that hurt. "Are we really going back to Jenica's today?"

"It was fun," Blitz says. "But it didn't feel quite right. Did it for you?"

I want to collapse with relief. "No. I missed Betsy something awful."

"They were killing each other for the sake of doing it," Blitz says. "I've had trainers like that. They think it's noble to sacrifice your body." He stretches his arms and winces. "I'm the first to want a hard, solid workout, but being unable to function the next day is no good in my business."

"Or getting injured," I say. "That would be the worst."

"Yeah, we were pushing it," Blitz says. "So, okay, we'll figure something else out."

"Even if that means you never get to see your super fan Weeza again?" I tease.

"I'll have to live with that." He drops another kiss on my hair.

"To the bath?" I say.

Blitz nuzzles my neck. "Definitely."

After an hour's soak, among other things, we start to feel human again. Blitz calls up a simple breakfast with healthy pressed juice and carbs, and we prepare to head to Dreamcatcher for the wheelchair ballerina class.

"You think BD will be there today?" Blitz asks. "Or did he get enough charge out of his outburst on Friday?"

I slide my Crocs on over my tights. "I honestly don't know. Danika should have security there by now. And presumably she has a restraining order in place."

"He still hasn't seen our gray car," Blitz says. "I could put a mustache on you."

I hold up my hands. "No need. I'll just wear sunglasses."

"So not fun," he teases. He calls down to the concierge to have the car brought around.

I shove my dance shoes in my bag. I don't really know what I will do if Denham is there again. He shouldn't be, if the order is in place.

"All set," Blitz says. "Let's go dance with your daughter!"

The idea of Gabriella being there makes me anxious. Denham has seen the pictures of me as a young girl. They were hanging in the halls. But that was a long time ago. Surely he won't remember them well enough to recognize Gabriella in them.

Although it's possible he could recognize something about himself. She has his eyes. Seeing him again confirmed it for me.

We head downstairs, where the gray Mazda waits. Blitz pulls a ball cap low on his face. With his sunglasses, he isn't recognizable. I wrap my head in a floral scarf and put on my own pair. Now I see why celebrities look like they do.

We drive in silence the short distance to the academy. Blitz approaches it slowly, watching for the green truck.

It doesn't take long to see it.

"Shit, he's right there," Blitz says. He makes an abrupt right on a side street to avoid driving past him.

"You think he saw us?" I ask.

"No," Blitz says. "He was fiddling with something on the sidewalk."

"He was out of his truck?"

"Yeah, kneeling on the ground."

We circle the block and approach Dreamcatcher from the other direction. The green truck is on the opposite side now. Denham is still sitting down low.

"What is he holding?" I ask.

"It's one of those construction-sized measuring tapes on a reel," Blitz says. "He's measuring something."

We turn into the drive, but I keep my face angled away. "Did he see us?" I ask.

"He glanced up, but he didn't recognize us in this car," Blitz says. "He looked right back down again."

"Did you figure out what he's doing?"

"The end of his measuring tape was the corner of the parking lot," Blitz says. He drives around to the back of the building and parks. "I'm guessing he's making sure he's outside the zone of the protective order."

"Is it that small?"

"I talked to Jeff about it when I was in LA. He didn't think we had enough evidence of a threat to get one, but that was before baby daddy decided to go nuts at a place with children. In Texas, it's typically two hundred yards."

"So a couple football fields," I say.

"Yeah."

"How could they have served him?" I ask. "He doesn't have an address."

"Jeff said he's on probation," Blitz says. "Most likely a stipulation of his probation is to maintain contact with an officer. They could serve it."

"Would getting one violate his probation?" I ask.

"I could call Jeff and ask," Blitz says.

"That's okay," I say. "Danika might know."

"I doubt we'll be able to get in the back door today without calling her," Blitz says.

"Looks like she has somebody back there." I point to the backstage exit.

Sure enough, a familiar tall man is there. Ted!

We walk up to him. "Fancy seeing you again," Blitz says. "I was just too good-looking to pass up."

Ted snorts. "They called and asked for me, since I already knew the place. I rotate with another guy, front entrance and back."

"Is this door locked?" Blitz asks. "Because lover boy is out front measuring how close he can get."

"We're aware," Ted says. "The funny thing is, we don't even have an order yet. They're still working on proving the threat. He's just being careful."

"Really?" I say. "Even after he went crazy last week?"

"Yeah, the owner wasn't able to convince them," Ted says. "I think they are getting some big-gun lawyer to file it now. Some dude named Claremont."

"Bennett," I say, and Blitz nods. Bennett built

Dreamcatcher Academy for Danika. He has lawyers on top of lawyers.

Ted turns to unlock the backstage door. "Buzz me if anything happens in there."

"Will do," Blitz says with a mock salute.

We hurry to Studio 3, where Janel is already working with Daisy and Marissa.

"Good morning," Janel says as we come in. "Small group so far this morning. Everybody's late or skipping."

I set down my bag. "Did anyone call to say why?"

"No," Janel says, adjusting Daisy's arms. "I didn't hear anything."

By the time we've changed into dance shoes, two more girls have arrived. But no Gabriella.

Halfway through class, Blitz comes up and says, "Did anything seem off with her on Thursday?"

I shake my head no.

"Why don't you go ask Danika about her?"

I nod. The girls are busily working on how to hold formation during a turn, so I head out into the hall and walk toward the front foyer.

Another security guard stands between the two entrances, looking out the floor-to-ceiling glass windows that make up the front of the academy. I realize how vulnerable we are, so open and easy to see in.

"Everything okay?" I ask him. "I'm Livia, the girl he's stalking."

The man nods in acknowledgment. "He just got served the order," he says. "The officer is still there, making sure he complies."

I glance out. I can't see Denham's truck, as it's too far down the street, but Denham himself is picking up his measuring tape. A squad car is parked directly in front of the academy.

I back away before he can look this direction. It's a good distance across the parking lot, and he shouldn't be able to see me clearly, but I don't want to take that chance.

Suze is at the front desk, and I wave as I pass. Then I stop and turn back to her. "Did Gwen call about Gabriella?" I ask. "She's not in class."

Suze sifts through her notes. "I didn't talk to her, but she left a message for Danika to call her. Maybe she's sick."

"Thanks," I say. "Is Danika back there?"

"I think so," Suze says.

I push through the doors to the recital hall. Danika's office is just inside. She sits at her desk, tapping on her keyboard.

I poke my head in. "Hey," I say.

"Hello, Livia," she says. "I take it you came in the back way? Your *friend* is out front."

"Yeah." I sit on the chair opposite her. "I hear you got the protective order."

"Finally. The officer who came didn't write up enough to get it through. We had to push it with Bennett's lawyer. But they got it done."

"Did he have a probation officer to notify him?"

"Yes, but we didn't want to wait on that. He was standing right out there. We got it rush-served. Anything for a price," she says.

"How far away does he have to stay?"

"We got three hundred yards, which is the maximum. But that's just for our property. He can still follow you."

"I know," I say. "Blitz doesn't want an order in the public record with my name on it."

"That makes sense. You practically have to give up your firstborn child to get one done."

I freeze, my breath catching.

Danika quickly says, "I'm sorry. That was a horrible thing to say."

"That's okay," I say. "It's just an expression."

She reaches across the desk to grasp my hands. "I think of you as a daughter, Livia. Please know that if you need anything, you can talk to me."

I'm not sure I can think of Danika as a mother, but I nod. "I came to ask about Gabriella," then quickly I add, "and Valerie. They aren't in class today."

"I'm not sure about Valerie," she says. "But Gwen heard about the altercation Friday and has put a hold on Gabriella's enrollment until it blows over."

"What?" My heart accelerates. "He didn't even come here on her day!"

"Gwen has some concerns," Danika says. "She isn't the only parent who has pulled her child out over that incident. I've lost about ten students."

I can't believe it. Just like that, Gabriella is out of my life.

Because of Denham!

"I'm so sorry," I say. "I shouldn't have come back here once he found me."

"I'm really not sure it would have helped. He comes here whether it's your day or not. He sat out there yesterday while we tried to get the order done."

"You think Gabriella won't even do the private lessons?" I ask.

Danika lets go of me and sits back in her chair. "It's interesting, Livia, that you and Blitz have taken such an interest in her. What motivated you to do that?"

My face flushes hot. I fumble with my answer. "Blitz saw a lot of potential in her when they did the video. She's really expressive."

Danika nods. "Well, that is true." She slides a few of her papers around. "I'll let you know if she decides to come back. I would assume her private lessons are also canceled for now. But I can check if you would like."

"Okay, thank you," I say. But I already know the answer. If Gwen doesn't want Gabriella to come to class, she won't want her to come to the academy at all.

Denham is costing me my daughter.

I have to do something.

## Chapter Twenty-One

I walk slowly back to class. It seems so forlorn in the studio with only four girls. I can't believe Gabriella is gone. I worked so hard to get her here.

I stand outside the window a moment. They can't see me there, as the window is a mirror on their side. Blitz is busily helping Janel show the girls a new routine. There's still twenty minutes in class.

I don't second-guess what I have to do. I march straight back down the hall, through the foyer, and am out the door before anyone can even say anything.

The police officer is still by his squad car, writing something on a notepad.

I can't see Denham, but I know where he is. I make it to the sidewalk and look down. Sure enough, he's moved another block to get outside the three-hundred-yard protective zone.

"Can I help you, Miss?" the officer asks as I pass, but I hold up my hand. Nothing is going to stop me from talking to Denham. I'm so angry. So absolutely outraged at what he has cost me. I can't believe I ever loved him. He's my biggest, worst, most absolute enemy at this moment.

Denham messes with the orange reel. Piles of kinked-up measuring tape are resisting going back on the roll. My ballet slippers are whisper quiet, so I'm right up at him when he notices me.

I shove his shoulders. "What is wrong with you? Why can't you just leave me alone?"

His face is smug. "Y'all are mighty jumpy in there for people who don't have anything to hide."

"You went crazy in there! Shouting and carrying on like a psycho. Of course Danika called the police."

Denham sniffs, his attention back on rolling up the reel. "I aim to find my baby girl."

"She isn't at Dreamcatcher," I say. At least now it's the truth.

"Then I reckon you better get right on with telling me where she is so I can be on my way. We don't have to have a thing to do with each other." He shakes the reel hard to knock out a kink in the tape. "I'm over all that, Miss Fine and Dandy."

"You cannot mess with her life," I say. "That isn't fair. You haven't been out of jail more than a few months at a time anyway. What is she supposed to do when you go back in?"

The tape unsnarls and rolls up, snapping against the case.

"I'm a changed man. I got obligations now. I intend to live up to them." He gives me a dark glance. "Not pawn them off on somebody else."

My head wants to explode. He thinks I wanted to give up my baby?

"I had no choice," I hiss. "I was fifteen with a father who was off-the-rails angry." I step forward and poke him again, making an indentation in the black leather jacket. "You were the one who wasn't there."

"I believe your father took care of that," he says calmly. The reel hangs loosely by his side.

"You didn't even try," I say. "You didn't show up at school. You weren't anywhere. I was stuck with what you did."

I want to cry now. I've never thought this through before. As angry as I had been at Denham, he was the best thing that had happened to me. And even though I never should have been with him in the first place, I had lost him and any help he would have given me with the baby. Maybe even finding the strength to keep her.

"You have no idea what my life became," I say. "It was horrible."

"Aww, Livia. Damn. I know. Mine was shit too. On the street. Trying not to starve. What was I going to do? Sixteen and your brother to boot. I had caused enough trouble for you." He tosses the reel in the back of his truck. The sound of it landing in the metal bed rings down the quiet street.

"I had nobody. And I was stuck. At least you could escape." I swipe my hands at the tears on my face.

"Come here." Denham wraps his arms around me. "We can fix this. You and me. Get our daughter. We can work this. See our baby grow up."

"She's got a family," I say. "She's happy."

"So you do know where she is," he says. "I knew you were smart like that. Is she close? Could we go see her now?"

I turn back to Dreamcatcher. The officer is standing there, watching us.

"I can't do that," I say. "She has a family. I just can't."

I pull my arm from Denham and try to walk away, but he follows.

"Livia, we can do this together. I know we can. I got father's rights. I'll let you see her whenever you want. Your guy's got money. Maybe he can get your rights back too. It'll work. You just have to believe."

I shake my head and walk faster. I won't do that to Gwen. I won't.

Denham grabs my arm again, and this time I forcibly shake him off. "Stop!" I say. "I won't be a part of this!"

I don't realize how close we are to the parking lot until Ted starts running down the steps. "Stay away from her!" he shouts.

This gets the officer in action. "You're violating the protective order," he roars at Denham.

Denham reaches for me again. "Livia, it's not too late to fix this thing." His hand closes on my arm.

I scream and whip myself away to get free.

Then everything is a blur as the officer and Ted both converge on Denham. I walk backwards, stumble, and catch myself as Ted tackles Denham. The officer turns Denham over and handcuffs him. He's followed me into the protective zone. I've made things worse.

Everything is so much worse.

# Chapter Twenty-Two

I run back to the building. Suze is standing by the windows, her blond hair bright, her face etched with worry. "Are they arresting him?"

I can't answer, gasping and trying to breathe, half crying. "Can you get Blitz?" I manage to ask.

"I gotta tell Danika what's going on first," she says, and takes off in the wrong direction, toward the office.

I turn and lean against the glass. Denham is on the ground, his cheek smashed against the sidewalk. Ted stands a few feet away. The police officer is talking into a headset. His hand is on Denham's back.

He's so screwed. On probation. Protective order. Violated. He'll go back to jail. It's my fault this happened. I led him right into the zone.

Danika rushes into the foyer, Suze on her heels.

She sees me and stops. “Did he come in here? Are you hurt?”

I’m crying too hard to speak but shake my head no.

“Stay here,” she orders and takes off down the steps for the parking lot. Suze puts her arms around me. “It’ll be okay. You want me to get Blitz now?”

I nod.

She moves away.

But she’s only gone a moment when the lights blink. God. The class transition. Everyone will come out and see a handcuffed man on the ground. More students will drop out. The other wheelchair girls. They might cancel the class for good. Gabriella will never come back. I’ll never see her again.

I dash out the door. “Let him go!” I shout. “Please! The kids are coming! They can’t see this!”

When I get to the huddle of people, Danika turns to me. “He’s violated the protective order,” she says. “This isn’t a choice anymore.”

“I led him down the sidewalk,” I say, frantic now. “Please, don’t arrest him. Everyone is going to see!” I kneel down next to Denham as if I can shield the world from spotting him.

But it’s too late. Cars start pulling in, parents bringing the next round of dancers. Kids start filing out the doors, leaving their classes.

Some of the parents hesitate, holding on to their children and hanging back on the steps. One or two of the cars slow down to turn, then drive right on by when they see the man on the ground.

"That's more emails," Danika says. She looks down at Denham. "Are you *trying* to destroy my dance studio?"

"I just want my daughter," Denham says, his cheek still pressed to the pavement. "That's all I want."

"Quiet," the police officer orders. "I'm waiting on backup," he says to Danika. "This was just supposed to be a serve." He looks down at me. "I'd really prefer you stay away, Miss. I saw him harassing you."

"He wasn't..." I say, but trail off. There is no way to explain the complicated events that led to this moment.

"I'll get in the car," Denham says. "I won't cause any trouble."

"Boy, you have already caused a lot of trouble," the officer says.

"He'll do it," I say quickly. "I know him. Just let him get in the car. Don't scare everyone."

"I'll help," Ted says.

The officer peers over at Ted. "And who are you?"

"My hired security," Danika says.

"All right," the officer says. He pulls Denham up by the handcuffs. "Into the car."

Denham stands. The officer and Ted lead him over to the vehicle. When he's safely inside and the door closed, my hands start to tremble. It's too much. All of it. I wish I had never met him, never talked to him, never let him near me.

I wish he had told me he was my brother, and we'd just been friendly and graduated from the same school. Or even that he hated us all along and ran off with his parts-stealing friends.

The sidewalk bites into my knees. I want to get up and go back in the academy, but I don't have the strength. The class yesterday. The stress today. I can't handle it.

A breeze picks up the loose tendrils around my face, but I can't even lift my arm to push them away. I just want to lie down and do nothing, think nothing, be nothing.

I know when Blitz comes out because I feel his arms around me. "Come on, Princess," he says. "They've got the bad guy."

I want to say that he isn't the bad guy. That I am. That I led him to all of this. I pursued him when we were young. And I led him to this arrest. It's me. All me. I'm the worst thing to happen to *him*.

When I don't move, Blitz scoops me up and

carries me back to the academy. We pass everybody, the wheelchair girls, Janel, Suze.

I keep thinking each day that this is the worst day, but it just keeps happening. Bad day after bad day. This nightmare won't end.

Blitz carries me down the hall to the storage room. It's our happy place, dimly lit from the light coming in the high windows, rays landing on costumes and sparkly hats. He sets me on a stack of mats.

"Talk to me, Princess," he says.

"He knows I know where Gabriella is," I say, gulping air.

"That's okay," Blitz says, smoothing loose hair back from my forehead. "That's different from knowing where she is."

"But I can't even see her anymore. Gwen removed her from the academy." More fat tears roll down my face.

Blitz lets out a gush of air. "That's tough. Do you know where they live?"

"Yes, but I can't exactly show up there." I throw up my hands. "Hello, Gwen, we stalked you all the way to your house to force your daughter to do a dance lesson!" My voice is shrill. I feel on the verge of hysteria.

"We can handle it delicately. We can say that we

agree that the academy isn't safe and we have a new location." His voice is calm, but this only upsets me more.

"Do you know how crazy that sounds?" I cry. "I just have to accept that I've screwed up. As soon as I went on your show, I put everything at risk."

Blitz holds my head, his palms on both my cheeks. He bends down until he's looking right in my eyes. "No, Livia. When you went on my show, you saved everything. You saved us. You saved me. And we're going to make this work."

"He'll tell everybody," I say. "Gwen will find out. God. It's over."

Blitz drags me against him and holds me tight. "Not if he's on our side," he says.

I hold my breath for a moment. I couldn't have heard him right. "What do you mean?"

"Let's go bail him out of jail. Get him a lawyer. Clean him up. Let's help him, and work out a deal we can all live with. You. Him. Gwen. She had to know this day might come. They didn't have a signature for a father. Did you ever look to see who your dad wrote down on the birth certificate?"

"I did." I force out a laugh. "Engelbert Humperdinck."

"The singer?"

"Yeah. Dad was always fascinated with his name."

"Well, that should have been a red flag for the adoption agency," Blitz says. "For Gwen. They ignored it. They'll know they did."

"They let it go, I guess. I don't know what Dad told them. We'd have to ask him."

"This is great, actually. The sort of thing a lawyer can build a case on." Blitz lifts me up and sets me back on the ground. "Let's call Jeff and have him refer somebody local to help us out. Then we can go bail out your baby daddy."

I follow him back to Studio 3 to change out of my ballet slippers. I don't know if helping Denham is the right thing. But it's a plan. It's something.

## Chapter Twenty-Three

By mid-afternoon, Blitz has secured a lawyer to meet us at the city jail to bail out Denham. His bond was set by the judge right after lunch, so it's just a matter of heading there to pay it and get him out.

We take the gray car to the courthouse. The lawyer said we won't be allowed back to see Denham, but he assured us that he'll meet with him and make the necessary arrangements.

"Are we liable for what happens to him if he does something once he's out?" I ask Blitz as we wait on a stiff row of chairs in a waiting area.

"I don't know. I've never bailed anyone out before," Blitz says. He holds my hand in both of his.

I smooth my simple black skirt and soft sweater. I've tied my hair back, trying to look as plain as possible. Blitz wears his sunglasses so he won't be spotted at a courthouse, casual in jeans and a sweater.

The room is large and filled with anxious people. I'm pretty sure I'm the only person in the room without a tattoo. One very tattooed grandmother watching a passel of small children talks with exasperation into a cell phone until an officer asks her to put it away or step outside. She tosses him an angry look, but shoves it in her bag.

A girl keeps staring at Blitz. I keep an eye on her, worried she has recognized him, but she is careful not to meet my gaze.

A man in a sharp navy suit comes out of a door and looks around. He spots me and Blitz and approaches. "Benjamin," he says, holding out his hand. "I'm Jeremy Trudeau. Let's go back to a private room to discuss the situation."

We stand up right as the officer barks "No cell phones" again. The room jumps. Must be the grandmother. I sympathize with her, probably having to wait on one of the parents of all those children.

We follow Jeremy through the door, held open by a uniformed officer. We go down a quiet hall and turn into a small stark room with only a table and a few plastic chairs.

Jeremy sits on one side, and Blitz and I settle in across from him.

"I had a conversation with Denham Young, and he says he doesn't want your help unless you're going to tell him the location of his daughter," Jeremy says. "We put together a provisional agreement." He pulls a sheet of paper out of a briefcase. It's covered with handwritten notes in tiny print. Denham's signature is at the bottom.

"That's all he wants? Her location?" Blitz asks.

"Yes. I came up with some demands for your side of the agreement given your concerns for the adoptive mother."

I sit forward on the chair. "What are they?"

"To approach the adoptive mother prior to requesting visitation with the child. To handle it privately, rather than involving social services. And to allow the birth mother equal access to the child."

Blitz nods. "What did he say?"

"He was okay with all that."

"Is he okay?" I ask. "How did he seem?"

Jeremy sits back in his chair. "Edgy. Anxious."

"Not angry?" I ask.

Jeremy shakes his head. "I didn't get that from him. He did ask about his truck. Seems everything he owns is in it."

"Did you tell him we'd take care of it?" Blitz asks.

"I did," Jeremy says. "He'll get his keys back from Admitting when he's freed."

"Will he just walk out?" I ask.

"Yes and no," Jeremy says. "We have to speak to his probation officer. And we'll need to have a place for him to stay. He'll also have to jump through some hoops about looking for employment here in town. Normal aspects of his probation, but particularly critical now that he's been in trouble again."

"It was my fault," I say. "I led him right into the protection zone."

"We explained that to the judge," Jeremy says. "I was here when the bond was set."

"So what's next?" Blitz asks.

"Either my office or yours can get him a residence," Jeremy says. "Someplace semipermanent so he can receive correspondence. We'll pay the bail, and he'll sign an agreement with me that I represent him."

"Sounds good. Do we sign this thing?" Blitz asks, pointing to the paper.

"We'll keep it informal as long as possible," Jeremy says. "You sure you want to take this on? You can walk away. With the probation and his priors, he'll get another six months, easy."

Blitz glances at me. "No, we have the bigger issue to settle. The child."

Jeremy nods. "I'm not a family lawyer," he says, putting the paper back in his briefcase. "But I'll get him in a position where you can move on that." He snaps the case closed. "But I'll tell you, if he does anything else, I'd drop him like a hot potato. You don't need that publicity on your head."

Blitz nods. "Understood. You going to go get him now?"

"You want to transport him?"

"No," I say. "Just let us know where he'll be staying. We'll meet up with him there."

"I'll have my people arrange it the moment we walk out of here," Blitz says. "They'll send you the address to get the probation officer to approve."

Jeremy stands and extends his hand. "That sounds good. I'd say you're crazy, but I guess you know what you're doing."

Blitz shakes his hand. "We don't, but then, who really does?"

Jeremy nods and moves to the exit. "You know where to find me."

He raps on the door and an officer opens it. Jeremy heads farther down the hall, and we go back to the waiting room.

"Should we stay here?" I ask.

"I guess not," Blitz says. "I need to call my assistant to arrange for BD's room and board. Probably can't do it here with the hounds monitoring our phone use."

Another officer opens the door to the waiting room.

And we are not prepared for what we see there.

## Chapter Twenty-Four

"Papá?" Blitz says, incredulous.

Blitz's father stands in the middle of the room, his face angry, his arms crossed. No one is paying any attention to him.

When he sees Blitz, he says, "I always knew I'd be down here eventually for one of you boys." His voice is gruff. He gets out his wallet and looks around. "You need me to bail you out?"

Blitz lets out a strangled laugh. "I didn't get arrested. How did you know I was here?"

"Your mother follows Tweeter or Nitwit or whatever it is," he says. "Apparently everybody's talking about how you are at the San Antonio jail. She made me get down here right away."

He sees a woman sitting behind a wall with a

small glass window. I guess he figures she's the one to pay to get Blitz out because he heads that way.

Blitz reaches out and grabs his arm. "I'm not in jail," he says. "I was here to help someone who got arrested."

They keep talking but I survey the room in a blind panic. Who recognized him? Was it that girl from earlier?

I despise that Blitz Burn hashtag and wish it would die a terrible social media death.

The girl isn't here anymore. Nobody seems to care, absorbed in their own drama. Moms, girlfriends, buddies, all with the same grim expression. The grandmother has also left.

I pull out my phone to see what is happening, but then I feel the eyes of the officer boring into me. Right. They don't want anyone using one. Now I see why. Compromised privacy.

"Livia?" Blitz finally gets my attention. "You ready to go?"

"You might want to rethink just walking out," his dad says. "There's a mob out there ready to take your picture."

Blitz stares at the door. "Really?"

"Out on the street," he says. "They didn't know who I was, but one step and you'll be all over those little newspapers your mother picks up at the grocery store."

We sit down in a mostly empty row. "What do we do?" I ask Blitz. "They'll recognize you no matter how we try to hide you."

"There's bound to be a back way," Blitz says. "Let me go ask and see."

He heads over to the woman behind the glass. I'm alone with his dad. I straighten my skirt self-consciously.

"You stick by my boy," his dad says. "That's something."

I don't know how to reply to that, since technically right now he's sticking by me. So I just give him a quick nod.

"Quite a life you're walking into." He looks around the room. "You sure you're up for it?"

"I've been up for it all along."

He leans forward, bracing his elbows on his knees. "Ben is an all-right boy," he says. "I guess if he's hung on to you this long, it's going to work. Nobody else has ever lasted a week."

This is probably as good as it gets in terms of praise from Blitz's father.

"He's a great man," I say. I avoid adding, "*Despite his father.*"

David seems anxious. He taps his thumb on his knee, a gesture I've seen Blitz do.

"I know I'm not the most pleasant person to be around. But I do try. Renata wouldn't have stayed around if I didn't. So if you need anything, Renata and I are happy to help out."

My jaw drops open and I have to think to close it. "Thank you," I say.

He sits back, as if he can relax now that he's gotten past that.

As Blitz comes for us, and his dad stands up and holds out his hand as if to help me up too, I realize he cares about his son. He's here. He can't be all bad.

"They won't escort us out the back themselves," Blitz says. "But the lawyer can take us out that way. We'll just wait on Jeremy." Now he's looking around the room too, wondering if anyone is covertly taking his picture.

We sit down again, feeling obvious and vulnerable. Blitz turns his back to the officer and covertly pulls his phone out. Then grimaces. He shoves it back in his pocket.

"Bad?" I ask.

"More than bad," he says. "I'm trending. Everyone's trying to guess my crime."

His dad snorts. "Can I send them some ideas?

That blue pantsuit you wore on your last show is bound to be illegal in most states."

Blitz laughs and pounds his dad on the back. "You watched it!" He settles back and takes my hand. "Yeah, my wardrobe girl probably needs to rein it in."

He seems happy and relaxed, despite the circumstances. I don't have a Twitter account, and I wouldn't dare comment on the situation even if I did. But I wish I could Tweet the truth.

*Blitz Craven is only guilty of being a nice guy. #ForgetTheBurn*

~*~*~

AFTER AN HOUR'S WAIT, BLITZ'S DAD DECIDES TO take off. "They don't know who this old fart is anyway," he says. He looks at me. "You want to come with me rather than get caught with this crazy fool?"

"They'll recognize her, I think," Blitz says. "Unless you're tired of waiting."

"No, I'll stay," I say. "Thank you, though."

David pats Blitz on the shoulder. "Be careful out there," he says. He gives me a nod. "Make this rascal come see his old man every once in a while."

"I will," I say.

When he opens the door, the crowd noise is

tremendous. Flashes go off until someone yells, "It's not him!"

A whistle blows, people shout. There's a foyer between this room and the outside door, so we're buffered against the crowd out there. Nobody is close enough to see in. We can't see them either. Thank goodness.

It's another hour before Jeremy peeks through the hallway door again. "I've got him," he says. "You guys can come this way."

As we stand up, I whisper to Blitz, "What does he mean by he's got him?"

Blitz shrugs.

But when we get in the hall, it's clear. Denham is there, shrugging on his jacket and shoving things in his pocket from an envelope.

"Hey," he says.

Another uniformed officer follows us as we walk down the hall.

Denham doesn't waste any time. "So when do I get to see her?" he asks me.

I glance over at the lawyer.

"We've got some things to arrange first," Jeremy says. "You need a temporary address. Check in with your probation officer. We need to contact the birth mother."

Denham cuts him off. "Livia, shut this clown up.

When can I see her?"

Blitz steps up as if to speak, but I hold up my hand.

"We have to talk to her mother first," I say. "She has no idea about any of this. She doesn't know who I am."

Denham stops walking. "What do you mean? Have you been seeing her or not?"

I glance at Blitz, then the lawyer.

"You don't have to go into this right now," Jeremy says. "Denham currently has no rights, and you should see a family lawyer before this moves forward."

The officer interrupts us. "Move along. This isn't time to chat."

We continue down the long snaking hall.

"I have the right to know if you've seen her," Denham says. "As her father."

"Yes," I say. "I have seen her."

He smiles at that. "My baby girl! Tell me what she's like. Does she look like you?"

"She does," I say. "Black hair. She's smart. And pretty."

"I bet she is," Denham says. "Does she dance like you? Tell me, does she go to that school? Is she a ballerina?"

I glance over at Blitz. His calm face gives me strength.

I take a deep breath, and just say it. “Denham, she’s in a wheelchair. She was in a car accident when she was three and she can’t walk anymore.”

Denham stops. The officer tries to move him forward, but Denham is rooted to the spot. “Our baby can’t walk?”

“No,” I say. “It’s been over a year. I haven’t talked to them about it, but I think if she were ever going to be able to walk, she would have done it by now.”

“Move ALONG,” the officer says.

Denham’s head is down, but his feet start moving.

We go in silence through a checkpoint, the sun finally coming in through glass doors at the back of the complex. This exit leads to a parking lot full of police cars.

“You can go out here,” the officer says. “Catch a taxi or have someone pick you up on the street. You can’t come back in this way.”

We’re unceremoniously dumped out onto the sidewalk.

He’s right, though. The lot is bordered on three sides by the complex. The street beyond the lines of cop cars runs with normal traffic. No bystanders. No cameras.

“Come on,” Jeremy says. “I’ll have my driver pick

us up. We can get you away from here until it blows over."

But as we move forward, Denham lags behind. I stop and turn to him. "Denham, you coming?"

"She's a cripple?" he asks, his voice still incredulous. "She's never going to walk?"

My throat constricts. "I had a hard time when I learned about it too," I say. "But she's a bright, sweet girl."

I try to take his arm to lead him with us, but he shakes me off.

"Denham, we have to go," I say.

He resists. "What am I going to do with a cripple for a kid?"

Now my chest starts to burn. "She's a perfect little girl."

Denham continues to stare at the ground, as if he can't wrap his head around this. "I can't do anything with that," he says. "That's too much responsibility." He still won't look me in the eye. "What'll everybody say when they see me with a kid in a wheelchair?"

We all stop to watch him. I'm so angry I want to hit him, hurt him like he is hurting my heart.

"You don't deserve her," I say.

He does glance up at me at that, just for a second. "Yeah," he finally says. "You're right about that."

He digs in his pocket for the keys to his truck. He

pulls a silver cross off the ring, banged up but heavy and well made. He tosses it to me.

I trap it against my chest and it falls cold into my palm.

"Give her that," he says. "It was my gramma's. Only thing I have of hers. Tell baby girl that her daddy was no good, and her daddy's momma was no good, but her great-gramma, she was good. Her name was Lucille. It's engraved on the back." He points at the cross. "Lucille Young."

I hold the heavy cross in my hand. "You aren't going to at least meet her?"

He shakes his head. "I'm gonna move on now. Thanks for getting me out." He peers up at the building, and the sun, squinting his eyes. "You'll do right by her. It's your way."

And with that, he takes off in long strides across the parking lot, through the cop cars, and turns down the street. We stand there, watching, until he's out of sight.

"That saves you quite a bit of trouble," Jeremy says.

I can't speak. I feel like my breath has been forced from my lungs.

Blitz gathers me up against him. "I'm here, Livia," he says.

"My driver is pulling up," Jeremy says. "Let's head

on to the street."

Blitz holds me tight as we follow the path Denham took through the cars. When we get to the sidewalk, a black Mercedes stops at the curb. I look up the street, trying to get one last glance at Denham, Gabriella's father, the love I once knew.

But he's disappeared, the tall buildings cutting off the view.

Just like that, this whole dark period of my life is over.

## Chapter Twenty-Five

By the time we're all the way back to the hotel, Blitz's social media team is working the #WhatDidBlitzDo hashtag, explaining how he was helping a hometown criminal get his life back on track. Somehow, they manage to move the activity over to #WhatWillBlitzDoNext and have people suggest nonprofits or causes Blitz could get behind.

By the end of the next day, it's all blown over. At least the jail part.

Danika calls to say Denham's truck is gone from the block. That's over too.

On Thursday morning, I pick at the breakfast Blitz orders up to our room. Normally we would be heading up to Dreamcatcher to have our private lesson with Gabriella. I have no idea where we stand on that.

"We can still go up to the academy," Blitz says. "Unless you want more punishment from Jenica. She's asking where we are."

"No, thank you!" I say, but I can't even muster a smile.

Blitz comes up behind my chair and lifts my hair to kiss my shoulder. "I think we should dance," he says.

I'm reluctant to go, sure I'll feel even more despondent when the hour for our lesson with Gabriella arrives and she isn't there. I pack my dance bag slowly so that we can get there after we would have danced with her.

We've just requested for the car to be brought downstairs when Blitz's phone buzzes. "It's Ted," he says.

"Is he still working as security for Danika?" I ask.

Blitz laughs. "Yes," he says. "And he sent a picture."

He holds up his phone. I'm not particularly interested in the shot until I see a familiar black head in a wheelchair, Ted kneeling beside her.

The message reads "My new client is wondering where her dance teachers are."

"Oh my gosh!" I say. "We have to go!"

I drag Blitz by the shirt to the elevator. He tries

to respond as we run down the hall and into the elevator to grab our car. We're still in the gray one.

Blitz races down the road to Dreamcatcher. I'm so glad we are staying close.

When we pull up, I instinctively look for the green truck, then shake that off. Denham is gone.

But Gwen's SUV is there. I don't wait on Blitz but run across the parking lot and burst through the doors.

Suze looks up. "They're in the studio," she says. "I think Danika is helping her."

I hurry down the hall. Blitz still hasn't caught up.

I slow down as I approach Studio 3. Ted stands outside the door. He nods at me.

"You're guarding her now?" I ask.

"Danika suggested it," Ted says. "Since her mother was nervous."

I glance in the window. Danika is taking Gabriella through the five arm positions. Gwen is inside today, sitting on the bench on the other side of the wall.

Blitz approaches. "Ted! You keep showing up like a drunk uncle!"

"Apparently you're enough trouble for a full-time gig," Ted shoots back.

"That I am." He takes my hand. "We going in?"

I nod and flash a smile at Ted as Blitz opens the door.

Gabriella looks up. "Benjamin! I have a special dance for you!" She rolls up to him.

"You do?" he asks.

"Livia taught it to me," she says. "Do you have the music?"

My throat is too tight to speak. I just nod and head to the audio controls in the corner.

As I plug in my phone to cue the music, I watch Gabriella circle around Blitz. Danika sits next to Gwen, and they say something to each other and nod. They are smiling.

My fingers tremble as I punch the buttons to find the song we chose for Gabriella's dance. I haven't lost everything. It's all here. Right in front of me.

The song begins and Gabriella gasps and rolls away from Blitz.

"The sparkle stick! Livia!" she calls out.

I grab one from the box on the floor and hurry it over to her. She takes it and strikes the opening pose, waiting for the first movement of the dance.

She turns the baton and tosses it into the air, catching it neatly. Gwen and Danika clap as Blitz cheers.

Danika catches my eye and nods. I wonder if she's figured it out, that Gabriella is my daughter. If that's why she brought Ted and convinced Gwen to come back to lessons.

I nod at her in return. Maybe we'll speak of it. Maybe we won't.

It doesn't matter right now as Gabriella does her dance.

She beams at Blitz as she turns her chair, spinning the baton. Light flashes off the sparkles that float inside the stick, sending a pattern across the mirror that reflects back into the room.

She's here.

She's beautiful.

She'll never know what happened. That her father rejected her. That her mother once thought she lived and loved in shame. Those things are not worth troubling her innocence and grace.

We'll have the lawyer add a record to her adoption contract giving my name so she can find me when she is eighteen, if that's what she wants. I don't want to get in the way of her life, her potential new father, or cast any shadow on how she grows up. I just want to see what I can.

The closing chords sound and Gabriella strikes her final pose. Blitz rushes to lift her from her chair, spinning her around and laughing, delighted at her dance for him.

There is no unhappiness here. Not now. It's all in my past.

I have been wounded. But I have survived.

And my life goes on, one more time, past the dark and into the light.

I have to believe the best is yet to come.

I hope you enjoyed *Wounded Dance*! While this book can stand alone, in the next book Wicked Dance, Livia is forced back into the glitzy world of *Dance Blitz*. Get book three or splurge for the entire Lovers Dance Boxed Set.

## Also by Deanna Roy

### The Forever Series

*A young couple reunites in colleges, four years after the death of their newborn.*

*Book one* Forever Innocent *is FREE on all venues.*

- Forever Innocent (Corabelle & Gavin)
- Forever Loved (Corabelle & Gavin)
- Forever Sheltered (Tina & Darion)
- Forever Bound (Jenny & Chance)
- Forever Family (Corabelle, Tina, Jenny)
- Forever Christmas (Corabelle & Gavin)

- Boxed Set: First Three Books
- Boxed Set: Final Three Books

- Stella and Dane (Standalone)

## The Lovers Dance Series

*A sheltered ballerina is lured into the life of a brash TV reality show star.*

- Forbidden Dance
- Wounded Dance
- Wicked Dance
- Tender Dance
- Final Dance

- Lovers Dance Boxed Set

- Billionaire's Dance (a standalone prequel)

## Other Books

- Conversations with Little Dude (Nonfiction stories with her son who was adopted from foster care)
- In the Company of Angels (A fill-in-the-pages baby record book for babies lost to miscarriage or stillbirth)
- The Magic Mayhem trilogy of action/adventure books for children ages 9-12.

---

## If you prefer your romances with no graphic love scenes or coarse language

You will love Deanna's pen name Abby Tyler. As Abby, Deanna writes funny, feel-good small-town romances with a recurring cast of feisty senior citizens and the couples they push together, by hook or by crook.

**Deanna** is the six-time *USA Today* bestselling author of romance and women's fiction.

She is a passionate advocate for women who have miscarried. She founded the web site Pregnancy-Loss.info in 1998 after the loss of her first baby and continues to run both online and in-person support groups for women who have endured this impossible loss.

She is a foster mom, an adoptive mom, and a baby loss mom. She lives in Austin, Texas, with her family.

Learn more about the author at
www.deannaroy.com

---

Join her email or text list for new release notices at
Deanna's List

facebook.com/deannaroyauthor
twitter.com/deannaroy
instagram.com/deannaroyauthor
goodreads.com/Goodreads
bookbub.com/authors/deanna-roy

# Sneak Peek of Wicked Dance

I hold my hands together tightly, sitting tall, mostly anxious that my skirt is short enough that I might give the cameras a crotch shot. My thighs ache from holding my knees together.

"How about those three lovelies from the show?" Doug, who is interviewing Blitz is smooth and overconfident. "Have you heard from them? Did they seem upset about the outcome?"

Blitz flashes a smile. "You'll have to talk to my lawyers about that one, Doug. You know women."

My face flames a bit. I glance over at Blitz's

manager Hannah to see if Blitz is behaving the way she wants. Her arms are crossed, a twisted smile on her face. She sees me looking at her, and moves her fingers to the corners of her mouth to remind me to smile.

Uggh. I plaster one on and turn back to Blitz. When he sees me, his expression shifts, like he realizes he's fallen into his old pattern. He sits forward again and reaches to find my hand.

Doug glances at Hannah, and I feel Blitz stiffen, his hand on mine painfully tight. I turn my attention to him, wondering what is going on.

And that's when I see them.

All three of them, dressed in flashy dresses, tons of cleavage, model-perfect hair, strolling in like they are the horsemen from the apocalypse.

The angry dethroned finalists from *Dance Blitz*.

I hope you enjoyed *Wounded Dance*! While this book can stand alone, in the next book Wicked Dance, Livia is forced back into the glitzy world of *Dance Blitz*. Get book three or splurge for the entire Lovers Dance Boxed Set.

www.ingramcontent.com/pod-product-compliance
Lightning Source LLC
Chambersburg PA
CBHW070750280626
47162CB00018B/2820

* 9 7 8 1 9 3 8 1 5 0 6 3 0 *